So They Went and Elected
a Jewish President

Tom Clancy

This book is dedicated to the Fischler family
formerly of Brooklyn, New York
who for many years gave me a second boyhood home
with trips to the Turkish baths
every Thursday night.

iUniverse books may be ordered through booksellers or by contacting:

iUniverse
1663 Liberty Drive
Bloomington, IN 47403
www.iuniverse.com
1-800-Authors (1-800-288-4677)

Because of the dynamic nature of the Internet, any Web addresses or links contained in this book may have changed since publication and may no longer be valid. The views expressed in this work are solely those of the author and do not necessarily reflect the views of the publisher, and the publisher hereby disclaims any responsibility for them.

ISBN: 978-0-595-52635-2 (pbk)
ISBN: 978-0-595-62687-8 (ebk)

Cover Design by Rex Poole

Printed in the United States of America

Acknowledgments

No book can be written, edited, proofed and produced in a vacuum. My thanks go to LaRee Simon who proofread the manuscript searching out inconsistencies and errors in logic, and also to my daughter, Susan, President of Rex Media, without whose publishing and computer skills the book could not have been produced.

My thanks also go to another daughter, Carolyn, a Project Coordinator at a major U.S. construction company, who typed the original manuscript at a mind-boggling, but accurate speed of 120 words per minute.

Two other daughters - Elizabeth and Madelyn also provided support on this and other writing projects.

Tevye, the milkman in *Fiddler on the Roof*, had five daughters. I don't quite measure up because I only have four.

Maybe next year…

Author's Note

This story has a light sprinkling of Yiddish words without which it would be impossible to portray the characters with any degree of realism. As a result of television, radio and newspapers, many Americans have become familiar with Yiddish terms like cockamamie, chutzpa, schlep. Yiddish expressions have a strong emotional quality and even when used in a critical sense always retain a touch of humor, as well as pity for the person being criticized.

Yiddish is not Hebrew. The latter is a sacred, liturgical language and has remained untainted by modern influences. Yiddish, on the other hand, an outgrowth of Hebrew, has been continually influenced by German, Spanish, Polish, Russian and several other languages. One might say that it is the modern day popular version of ancient Hebrew.

The Yiddish expressions used in this story are defined on the last page.

Jewish Humor

…Somewhat confrontational, sometimes critical, but always humorous. A few examples:

Two men are seated in a New York deli. The waiter approaches and one of the men asks for a nice glass of iced tea. The other man says: "That sounds delightful. Bring me a glass of iced tea, too."

The waiter takes the order: "Two glasses of iced tea."

As the waiter starts to go to the kitchen, one of the men says to him: "Waiter, make sure the glass is clean."

A few minutes later, the waiter returns with the iced tea and asks: "Which one of you wanted the clean glass?"

Leo Rosten

Calvin Trillin, commenting on his Jewish mother: "The remarkable thing about my mother is that for thirty years she served nothing but leftovers. The original meal has never been found."

Jewish view on when life begins: In Jewish tradition, the fetus is not considered viable until it has been accepted in a medical school.

A man calls his mother in Florida. "Mom, how are you?"

"Not too good," says the mother. "I've been very weak."

"Why are you so weak?" asks the son.

"Because," she says, "I haven't eaten in 30 days."

"That's terrible, Mom. Why haven't you eaten in 30 days?"

"Because," his mother answers, "I didn't want my mouth to be filled with food on the outside chance that you might call."

Principal Characters

The Parents of President David Fishman

Rose and Harry Fishman

The President's Cousins

Sylvia Fishman Steinberg and her husband, Saul

Rachel Fishman Schlotsberg, her husband, Herman,
and their daughter, Marsha

Hymie Fishman, his wife, Shirley,
and their son, Arnold

The Assassins

General Ali Moishe Karasek

Colonel Zumar Karam

Hassar

The Student Accomplice

Abu Aram (alias Izzy)

The Doctor

Doctor John Doctor

So They Went and Elected
a Jewish President
Tom Clancy

MAZEL TOV!

So They Went and Elected a Jewish President

1

When the news flashed across the television and computer screens of the nation and indeed, the world, that the Republican candidate for president of the United States had capitulated to the Democratic candidate and that David Fishman, U.S. senator from New York, had won the election, several hundred of Fishman's relatives sat around in kitchens, dinettes, steam rooms and kosher delis in New York, Miami, Los Angeles and a few other places, trying to decide whether or not to move to where the action was: Washington, D.C.

It was not an easy decision.

One and all, the president-elect's kin realized they were facing a monumental proposition, one that would be disruptive, expensive and risky. Sell the house, yank the kids out of school, quit the job (if they had one), sell the business (if they had one), and GO! There could be fame, fortune and excitement living in the nation's capital, but then again maybe only excitement. The economy had gone from bad to worse under the current Republican administration. Many of the president-elect's relatives were underemployed; some were unemployed; some were trying to run businesses in which the foot traffic had deteriorated to a passing shuffle of window shoppers who didn't have money to buy anything. So, taxes were cut! But if you weren't making any money, you weren't paying taxes anyway. And waiting for the trickle down economy was like lying on your back on a hard wooden bench while C.I.A. water torturers let droplets drip on your face.

Also, moving to Washington did not provide long term guarantees. The cool-headed ones among the relatives were quick to see that if they were going to "make it" it would have to be done in four years since they counted David Fishman's election as something of a miracle. Few believed it wise to count on another miracle in the form of a Jew being elected to a second term.

And what then? Sell the house, yank the kids out of school, get booted out of that high-paying government job, and go back to New York or Florida, or wherever, and start all over again. Exodus they all believed in, but Exodi? They weren't so sure.

The more sensible ones decided to stay put for the time being and if the economy turned up, perhaps they might be able to put some money away for a short tourist visit to Washington, D.C. It would be educational for the children and being relatives of the new president, or perhaps only friends of relatives, they could probably swing a tour of the White House conducted by the president himself.

Although sensible, some of them were obviously dreamers.

Sketched out on white tablecloths by huddles of relatives and in notebooks by high school and college kids, were the many branches of the Fishman family tree. Unlike the usual family tree that branches down from long-deceased ancestors, the tablecloth and notebook trees branched outward like overgrown Hanukkah bushes to embrace aunts, uncles, nephews, nieces, cousins and hangers-on. David Fishman was variously depicted as the taproot, or in some cases, the sturdy trunk.

Many in the family realized for the first time what it was like to be merely the eighth twiglet on the seventeenth branch way over on the far side of a Hanukkah bush. And if twigs and branches represented blood ties, given the multiplicity of weak and clogged arteries, it wouldn't take a tree surgeon to realize the bush was in danger of a heart attack. In this botanical tangle, whenever a tie to David Fishman could be traced, the relative in question was quick to point out that he or she had at some time been close in a *personal* way to David. In some cases, the truth was stretched, in others it split like a thirty-eight inch pair of pants wrestled onto a forty-four inch tochis. If, in fact, the relative had ever met David Fishman, a more likely scenario would have taken place in which David, as a young boy, while attending an older boy's Bar Mitzvah, might have been patted on the head by the relative and told to stop picking his nose and stand up straight.

*****

"Harry, I really think we should sell the store and move to Washington, D.C. After all, you're the president's father! You should be down there to help him run things."

Seated at the kitchen table in the small apartment over the store, Harry shook his head. "Rose, Rose. How many times do I have to tell you. I'm a small businessman. I don't know anything about running the government."

"Look at it this way, Harry. You've always been good at handling food, buying the inventory for the store, and generally running things like that. And with all the food and things they have to buy at the White House—they're entertaining guests constantly...perhaps you could help with some of that."

Harry shrugged, saying to himself: "That's possible. She may be right. But my specialty has always been chocolate bars, cigarettes, newspapers and sundries, and for important people who have important things to do, it doesn't sound like a well-rounded diet."

*****

So They Went and Elected a Jewish President

David Fishman had been born into a lower middle class family in Brooklyn, and after succeeding handsomely in New York politics, marrying Lisa Morrison, a New York socialite and daughter of a wealthy banking magnate, had drifted away from his extended family like a sleek white schooner escaping a floating mass of flotsam. He dearly loved them all, but he was a very ambitious and very, very busy man. The exceptions, of course, were his mother and father. But even then, his contacts with them were limited to phone calls and on occasion, a quick visit to the store. His wife never came. His parents were never invited to dinner or parties at his Park Avenue apartment. The easy explanation, agreed to by both the parents and the son, was that they couldn't take time away from the store.

David Fishman, of course, was too well-liked across the land to be termed a snob, but he had developed a wariness and aloofness characteristic of some men in high places. Even his close relatives, partly through shyness, and what they liked to think of as a certain feeling of independence, rarely pressed their attentions on him as he rose to higher stations in life.

And all of that was fine as long as he was *rising*, but now he had hit the top! Now the family sensed that the relationship deserved a hard second look. Now they had to face up to the fact that the power of office of their cousin, nephew, uncle, or whatever, could bring about profound changes in their lives. You could casually pass off that you had a relative who was in congress and go on waiting on customers in the store, but it was difficult to be casual when the relative was president.

In the year leading up to the election, Harry had found that when people became aware that he was the father of merely the Democratic *candidate* and the *underdog candidate* at that, they nevertheless came in droves to his candy store and lunch counter in Baldwin on Long Island. Many people drove hundreds of miles to glimpse the man who had fathered a national figure.

"Not all of them *buy*," Harry said to his wife as he stood behind the counter watching the surging crowds, "and it's annoying the way they keep shooting those flash cameras off in my face but I should complain when in just a few months, the business has tripled? And look at all the film we've been selling. *We* sell them the film, compact discs and batteries so they can take pictures of *us*. It's a natural!"

"I'm from the *New York Times*," one eager young man said as he stood in front of Harry's counter, camera in hand. "Let's have a picture. Put your arm around your wife. That's it. Good. Now can I have a double chocolate shake?"

"If you can promise the picture for the front page," Harry replied, "the shake is free; but if it's going back on page twenty, I'll have to charge."

Harry even added a line of cameras to his bulging display cases since obviously a lot of people came into the store who might want to take a picture of him and Rose but who didn't have a camera.

Harry Fishman was a simple man, one who had worked the long, tedious hours of a storekeeper all his life, and who believed that good things only come through hard work. He was proud of the fact that he had enlisted in the Navy in the Korean War and saw service for three years at sea. His fondest memories were of seeing his son graduate from Harvard Law School and seeing him elected to the United States congress. Bewildered by his son's meteoric rise, he was openly proud but inwardly dubious, wondering how such a thing could happen. He knew that *he* could never win or deserve national fame. What was there to him? Five-foot-three, a little on the heavy side, white hair, pretty good with figures, and he knew his business. A formula that fit thousands, maybe millions of elderly men in the country. And his wife, Rose, was cut from the same cloth. But their son, David, he was the miracle.

*****

As Harry swept the sidewalk in front of the store, he remembered the small candy store he and Rose had run in the Bronxville section of Brooklyn, until the crime and shabbiness had driven them, with their only son, David, out to a better neighborhood on Long Island.

On Merrick Road, on the opposite corner from St. Mark's Catholic Church, he and Rose had bought a larger store in which they combined a lunch counter, candy counter, magazines and sundries. The income had put his son through college and Harvard Law School and provided a modest, but comfortable living for the couple in the apartment above the store.

Harry loved the Sunday morning crowds that swarmed in from the church across the street after each of the Masses. He liked the business and the customers. In time, he found he had become acquainted with far more Catholics than Jews, and he also found that Catholics weren't bad after all, as long as you kept the conversation away from religion. He was also a bit awed at the astonishing craving of the Catholics who crowded his lunch counter for kosher hot dogs, kosher dill pickles, and potato knishes. He often wondered that if, as the saying goes, we are what we eat, the priests across the street maybe didn't know it, but their Sunday noonday congregation was a pretty good percent kosher.

So They Went and Elected a Jewish President

When his son became the presidential candidate, Harry, who had grown accustomed to a lot of Sunday Catholics, now found that every religion under the sun was coming into the store. Even Orthodox Jews came. But they usually slipped in the side door because they didn't want "to accidentally walk" in the shadow of the tall steeple of St. Mark's across the street.

And if any who entered the store wasn't aware that the owner was the father of a presidential candidate, the splash of American flags on the wall behind the cash register, surrounding a large picture of David, soon told them there was something a little different about *this* Mom and Pop store!

As the campaign heated up around the nation, the store began looking more and more like campaign headquarters. So flag- and poster-decorated was the store that some even thought it to be a polling place.

"Where do I go to register?" asked an elderly woman with a puzzled look on her face one day. "I can't find anyone in back who'll take my name and address, and if you don't move that lunch counter out, you'll never have room for the voting machines."

"Madam," Harry explained patiently, "this is only a store. We serve some food, magazines, and sundries, but we don't allow voting! However, if you're planning to vote for my son, on election day you can get a ride in one of the charter buses I'm arranging for, and after that, you will be brought back here for a free kosher hot dog and a nice glass of seltzer."

And so the crowds surged, calling for David Fishman Butter Cookies, flags of all sizes, and buttons with David's picture, until it all ended for Harry and Rose. Their son, they realized in shock had had the chutzpa to go and get himself elected!

By no later than eleven o'clock on election night, all of the network and cable TV computers showed that their son had racked up an unbeatable lead. The hired five-piece band played loudly on the street corner by the store as colorful crowds mingled in a mammoth block party. Even the weather cooperated, providing an unusually warm November night. The local fire department used two of their pumpers to block traffic from Merrick Road in the vicinity of the store. Even the young priests from St. Mark's joined in the celebration.

Harry and Rose were deliriously happy. At one point around midnight, they waltzed on the sidewalk, to the delight of the crowd. Still later, Harry danced around telling people that his next store was going to be six times as big.

Little did Harry realize that the night's event was destined to change his life as a storekeeper for a very long time.

Roger Halstead, standing in a relaxed position with his arms folded, pressed his rump back against the table as he faced a score of staffers in the conference room. He was exhausted after the long campaign. Halstead had been a senior adviser to David Fishman during Fishman's years as a senator and more recently, served as the Democratic party's principal strategist during the presidential campaign. There were more sleepless nights on airplanes than he could count, but he'd had to press on. The tousled hair and rumpled brown suit showed that he was casual about his appearance; nevertheless in matters of politics, he was disciplined, hardworking and loyal.

The meeting was being held in the "war room" on Connecticut Avenue in Northwest Washington, D.C., the incubator of the new administration.

The men and women in the room had all been active during the campaign and were now present to take on new assignments. They too, were exhausted with a kind of giddiness that comes from lack of sleep. However, each was willing to serve on a temporary team to carry out the post-election, pre-inauguration plans laid out by the president-elect. The motivation: hope for reward in the form of a high-level government job in the White House or other government agency after the inauguration, if they could only survive long enough.

"I have a long list of items," Roger said in opening, "so please bear with me. The first item involves security. As we are all acutely aware, the soon-to-be president is Jewish. This obviously raises a lot of concern. We need to take extraordinary precautions for his safety."

A hand went up. "Isn't that the bailiwick of the Secret Service and perhaps the CIA?"

"Yes, *but.* Frankly, the Secret Service and the CIA have been involved in a number of fiascoes recently. We can't completely rely on them. I'm alerting you to think about the problem although I admit there isn't much we can do to actively participate right now."

Footsore, Roger hoisted his fanny onto the table. "Let me tell you why I'm worried: our incoming president is a fitness buff, as you probably know. He rides his bicycle through crowded city streets in the mornings. Sometimes he even goes from one meeting to another on his bike later in the day because he claims it is a lot faster than bucking the city traffic. Limo's and taxis don't move through traffic any faster than other cars. Happily, although he has been a senator for five years, there have been no attempts on his life. As president, however, here in Washington, the situation could be very different. I expect he will be out riding early every morning. So the threat becomes very real."

"Why not teach the Secret Service to ride bikes?" one staffer asked with a chuckle and a broad smile through half-closed eyes.

Laughter.

Roger gave the speaker a long stare. "I know you meant that as a joke, but in fact, I have canvassed the Secret Service and they tell me that Fishman is *fast*. Very few agents can keep up with him. But it may work out because they've begun a training program. Any other suggestions?"

A hand went up in the back. "Why doesn't he get a stationary bike? Then he'll be safe riding inside the White House."

"He likes fresh air and the feeling that he's getting somewhere as he rides."

"Fresh air in Washington?"

Another hand went up. "Why don't the Secret Service agents ride motorcycles? They could easily keep up that way."

"Because," answered Roger, with an edge creeping into his voice, "can you imagine the noise and commotion from a bunch of motorcycles going through city streets at six A.M.? People would think Hell's Angels had arrived in town. Also, the noise would drown out the sound of anyone trying to take a potshot at him. Well, I don't think we're getting anywhere with this. So, on to another threat. There is a notorious foreign agent who may be after the new president. We don't know his name, only his initials: A.K."

Laughter.

"Damnation! Can't you guys in the front row take this seriously?"

"I want you to know that this A.K. guy, whoever he is, is dangerous."

A hand went up. "Where's this A.K. from? What's his nationality?"

"Don't know," Roger answered with a look of growing concern on his face. "He could be from any one of half-a-dozen countries in the Middle East. He might even be an Israeli."

"If he tries to enter the country, why don't they pick him up at Customs?"

"Not so easy," Roger replied. "Customs has been criticized for 'racial and ethnic profiling.' It's similar to the criticism cops get for excessive stopping of minorities on the highway. Several Middle East countries have complained. They even plan to retaliate. They say that if the practice doesn't stop, they will strip search American tourists. Yes, even little old gray-haired ladies will have all body cavities examined. It's just a form of harassment. So, as a result, our Customs agents have backed off. What's more, this guy, A.K., is said to carry about five different passports. If they're watching for an Arab, he pulls out an Israeli passport, and vice versa."

"Can't they tell if he looks more like an Arab than an Israeli?"

"Gimme a break," Roger answered, "seems to me those people from the Middle East all look a lot alike. So, this guy may well slip into the country undetected. And there are three or four other accomplices who might be coming: one from Libya, one from Iraq, one from Syria, and so on. Could be a bad situation. Well, again, we seem to be stymied for a solution right now, so on to another threat. This one comes from Fishman's family."

Every eyebrow in the room was raised.

"Let me explain. The new president has a large family spread around the country. Because of the recession, many need help with jobs and such. They may descend on Washington en masse."

"Have they got a parade permit?" one kibbitzer asked. Roger wearily stood up. He began pacing the floor. "Look, gang, you don't seem to be taking any of this seriously. If you think you're going to get government appointments after the inauguration, you'd better start getting serious. I know you're all giddy from exhaustion, but enough is enough."

This was followed by widespread apologies.

A hand went up.

"Yes, Jean, what is it?"

"Can't we do anything to help his relatives? I've heard that many of them have lost jobs and small businesses."

"Fishman says, and I quote: 'There'll be no nepotism in my administration.' He goes on to say that if any of his relatives are qualified for the jobs they are seeking, fine, but they have to do the paperwork and compete for the jobs like everyone else."

"But that paperwork you refer to, Roger, the government application, is mind boggling. You have to list education, experience, references, hobbies, psychological history, list of organizations you belong to, list of organizations you *don't* belong to... it's like writing a book."

"Sorry, Jean, but that's the boss's rule. Now for assignments: Jean, you and Mary team up on the Inaugural Address. Here are a few thoughts scribbled by Fishman. Tony, you get a list of Fishman's relatives. Remember, we want names and addresses of his extended family. George, you get in touch with the president-elect's parents on Long Island. Convince them to sell that store and move down here. Be as persuasive as possible. The president's parents should live in Washington to give the impression that the president is a family man with loving parents at his side."

"Will they live at the White House?"

"No way," Roger answered. "The new first lady would never allow that. She doesn't want her mother-in-law underfoot. Just find them a place nearby."

"Who's gonna pay for it?" George asked.

"They are. They ought to get a bundle from selling that store. I hear it's mobbed these days. It's a gold mine. Now Henry, where's Henry? Oh, there you are. Henry, you have a background in communications, right?"

"Right."

"I want you to arrange guest spots for the president-elect on the Today Show, Good Morning America, the Tonight Show, Meet the Press, and so on. It will give him a chance to lay out some of the details of his program, a chance to get support for his program and get a jump on the Republicans in Congress. It'll get the people solidly behind him."

"Right," Henry replied. Henry was a man of few words.

"Henry, tell me something. With that background you have in communications, I've never heard you utter more than one word at a time. Is that right?"

"Right."

"Well as long as you take care of it, I don't need a big explanation about how you're gonna do it."

"Right."

*****

"Hello. My name is George Evans. I'm calling from Washington. I'd like to speak to Mr. Harry Fishman. Is he there?"

"This is his wife, Rose. Let me transfer your call."

"Thank you."

Rose walked across the kitchen of the apartment and picked up the broom. She turned it upside down and banged the broom handle on the floor three times.

Downstairs, behind the counter, Harry picked up the phone. "A man from Washington wants to talk to you, Harry. He's on the line."

"Hello. This is Harry Fishman, father of the president-elect. Can I help you?"

"Mr. Fishman, my name is George Evans. I'm with your son's transition team. I'll be brief. We want you and your wife to relocate in Washington, to be close to your son."

"But I have a store to run. Besides, after he's in the White House, whenever I should want to see my son or he wants to see me, we'd only be

9

three, maybe four hours away by train...five hours by car...one hour by air. Thank you and goodbye."

"Mr. Fishman, just a moment, Sir. We think it is very, very important for you to live here in Washington during your son's administration."

"He can't run the government without me?"

"It's more of a family matter. We think it would look better if the president's parents were here on scene. You might even have lunch at the White House once in awhile. Wouldn't you and your wife like that?"

"Would it be kosher?"

"Your meals could be made kosher-style."

"Well, that's OK because my wife and I are not Orthodox. I sometimes even have a slice of bacon with my eggs in the morning. And, once in awhile, we even have pork tenderloin, always well-done that is, and..."

"Mr. Fishman, so you say you agree? You'll move down?"

"No. I didn't say that. What would I do for money down there? Maybe someone would help me get a job. Can I get a government job? Is that possible?"

"I kind of doubt it. But think of it this way: your son has married well and will have a nice salary as president. Perhaps he could give you and your wife an allowance."

"A father gets an allowance from a son? Listen, Mister Whatever-Your-Name-Is, I raised my son. I paid him all the way through college, and law school on top of that. And I'm not complaining, mind you, but what I typically look forward to from my son is the shirt he always sends me at Hanukkah, and the new wallet he always gives me on my birthday, with a dollar in it for good luck. More, I wouldn't want him to offer, and more, I definitely would not take."

In the following days, more calls came from Washington with a message that became a drumbeat: since Harry, in his early seventies, was well into retirement age, why, Washington asked, didn't he retire? Besides, wouldn't the father and mother naturally want to be near the son in Washington to aid in discharging the many social obligations of the new office?

Rose made it plainer: "Harry, let's sell this damn store and GO!"

So Harry put the business up for sale. Pressed for cash to finance the move to Washington, he found there wasn't much time to wait out the buyers; nor did Harry think it wise to delay since large crowds continued patronizing the store, making it look like a gold mine. He was secretly afraid that the business might taper off when people got used to the idea that he and Rose were the president's parents. "After all," Harry said aloud to himself, "how many pictures of the president's parents do people need?"

Potential buyers were sufficiently business-wise however, to know that the foot traffic was transitory, and when Rose and Harry left, so would many customers.

Harry finally sold the store at a price lower than he had hoped for since the buyers insisted on a price based on a "non-election year" sales volume. After the sale, he and Rose moved down, taking an apartment just outside of Washington in fashionable Chevy Chase. Harry knew they really couldn't afford it. It was way beyond their usual standard of living. Since he wouldn't be working any more they would be living off the cash received from sale of the store. It would last quite awhile, but not forever.

On the day before they moved down, while Rose and he were packing their possessions, Harry grew disturbed. What would he do with himself all day long in Washington? The first few weeks, maybe the first few months, would be fine, a nice vacation. But after that?

While they were having their last dinner in the apartment over the store, the couple looked at each other. Rose ate with gusto, as usual, but Harry, too upset over the selling and packing and moving, tasted a little and then put his fork down. He looked at Rose. "Tell me, what will I do all day down there in Washington?"

"Do? You'll be with me. You'll do what I do, I suppose."

"That's what I was afraid of," Harry retorted.

Rose began nibbling off Harry's plate. "Now look at it this way," she said enthusiastically, "we'll get all dressed up and go to wonderful dinner parties. I'll have gowns and cocktail dresses. There'll be black-tie functions, white-tie functions; you'll lose some weight and look good in tails or a tuxedo, whatever. We'll hobnob with important people. We'll go to some White House receptions and dinners. We'll meet important dignitaries from all over the world."

"That sounds very nice, Rose, but, receptions and dinners, can we make a *life* on that?"

"Well, I don't know about *you*," Rose replied, "but I've been waiting almost seventy years for a life like that!"

Saul, standing with a martini in his hand on the crowded side patio of the Indonian Ambassador's residence in Washington, was waiting for Harry to come back from the bathroom.

Saul Steinberg, cousin-in-law of the incoming president, looked quite tall and trim in his new tuxedo, a shock of wavy black hair tumbling onto his forehead and a slight touch of early gray showing at the temples. A woman who brushed by looked up giving him a lingering and admiring stare, which, although he appreciated, he ignored.

Saul and his wife, Sylvia, had come down from New York on a visit at the urging of Rose and Harry, the incoming president's parents. The Steinbergs had agreed to move to Washington as soon as they could find an apartment.

After each sip of his martini, Saul glanced restlessly back over his shoulder at the floodlit castle-like edifice that loomed behind him. He wondered about Harry. Harry had surely lost his way somewhere in the bowels of the massive building. Poor Harry. Saul hoped he had made it in time. The party was literally awash in liquids. They had seen a dozen waiters briskly shuttling trays covered with cocktails, and had seen half-a-dozen bartenders at three different bars on the side patio alone. They were surrounded by temptations for liquid *intake*, while artfully and somewhat diabolically concealed were any places for liquid *outgo*. Saul imagined that the people who frequented these parties either knew where the little room was or had the guts to ask. New to this way of life, Harry, and Saul too, had neither attribute.

Saul's wife, Sylvia, and Harry's wife, Rose, both elegantly dressed in fashionable cocktail dresses, moved gracefully through the milling throng. After sampling the buffet offerings on the side patio tables, they had drifted out to the back lawn to see if they might have missed any Indonian delicacies on the tables set up under the huge party tent behind the residence.

Saul fidgeted awkwardly alone, thinking they might all have a bit of fun at what seemed to be a nice party, his first embassy party at that, if they could only stay together. Where the hell is Harry, dammit? Saul muttered under his breath.

The occasion was a party being given by the ambassador of the Kingdom of the Indonian Islands. The tiny kingdom, located in the Banda Sea, along the Indonesian archipelago, was famous for its dark-skinned youthful naked Hupa dancers, its dawns, which came up like Mandalayan thunder, accompanied by startling flashes of silver lightning on a crimson horizon, and its world-renowned monkey chitlins soup. The Indonians had another name for the soup, but most people could tell by the gooey meat near the bottom of each bowl that it was a kind of chitlins. There wasn't any doubt about why the monkey population of the Islands suddenly dwindled when the soup first became popular in the early 1900's. Thus, importing and raising monkeys came to be one of the largest industries in the kingdom; another, naturally, being soup preparation.

The Indonian embassy staff in Washington were quietly forbidden visiting privileges to the National Zoological Park because of an unfortunate incident in the monkey house a few years earlier. The incident was one that all of official Washington had heard about, but never discussed. At least, when Indonians were within earshot.

Along the upper reaches of Massachusetts Avenue, in the wooded northwest section of Washington, the Indonian ambassador's residence was situated well back behind a stone wall that had two high iron gates. Fronting the avenue, the gates opened onto a semi-circular driveway that curved in tangent to the main entrance of the imposing floodlit mansion.

A large seal in the form of a royal blue shield was mounted atop the entrance gate. The official seal had been intricately designed to illustrate the weather, industry and culture of the island kingdom. Jagged silver streaks across the top symbolized the dazzling sunrises. An image of a monkey on the lower right depicted a major industry, soup preparation; and a small photo of a group of naked Hupa dancers illustrated the culture. Local Washington clergymen had fought unsuccessfully to have the 'pornographic display' removed, but the embassy prevailed by use of diplomatic immunity.

On that unseasonably warm evening in early December, most of the party had spilled out through the open doors of the palatial residence onto the side and rear patios, and even onto the back lawn part of which was covered by a huge colorfully striped party tent. At the beginning of the party, Saul and Sylvia had endured the formalities of the receiving line inside the residence, one which Rose and Harry missed by arriving late. As the party warmed up, the horde of glittering partygoers soon discovered that all of the bars were set up outside. Not only did this stem from the fact of having available a balmy evening, but also from an attempt on the part of the ambassador's frugal wife to save the cherished Persian rugs from whiskey stains and cigarette holes. She almost succeeded.

As Saul was standing there alone, feeling conspicuous, surrounded by clusters of gaily chatting people, none of whom he knew, but all of whom seemed to know one another, he had a sudden urge to strike up a conversation.

13

A middle-aged and distinguished-looking gentleman, of medium height, in a dark business suit, was standing alone a few paces away by the patio railing. Saul noted the man's bald but interesting head, its plateau-like pate encircled with close-cropped white fringe. The man's round face was elongated by a jutting, sharply pointed white van dyke.

Saul stepped over to strike up a conversation.

"Hello, I'm Saul Steinberg. How are you getting along?"

"Fine. Just fine," came the reply. The man smiled warmly, but then merely stood there holding his drink and looking up at Saul.

Saul tried uneasily to make some casual comment or other about the party when the man volunteered, "My name is John Doctor. I'm a doctor."

"I see. Then it's Doctor Doctor, is it?"

"Yes, that's right."

Silence.

"Aah... are you a doctor, Doctor? I mean as opposed to being a physicist or engineer or something..."

"Yes, I am in medicine."

"Oh, I see. Well then, are you...aah...a physician perhaps? I mean as opposed to being a specialist?"

"You mean general practitioner."

"Yes, that's what I meant. You know, like an ordinary doctor."

"Well, as I said, I *am* a doctor; however, more specifically, I'm a surgeon."

Saul knew he had made a terrible mistake striking up this conversation. Why weren't they talking about football? baseball?...anything. He glanced over his shoulder but still no sign of Harry. Saul thought he might as well keep trying awhile longer. "Football?" he asked. "How about that game Saturday?"

"Hate football. Never watch it. Watching sports is a waste of time."

How can you get annoyed at a guy, Saul thought, when he stands there with such a big friendly smile, even when the conversation borders on torture.

"Er...aah, what kind of surgery is your specialty? I'm assuming, of course, that surgeons do have a specialty."

Saul was getting desperate. He tried guzzling his drink so he could excuse himself to go for a refill.

"Oh yes, we tend to be a highly specialized lot," the doctor agreed happily. "Lately, I have been working in the field of organ transplants."

Saul nodded his head in a false attempt at approval. Where the hell is Harry? he asked himself for the hundredth time. He started edging towards the bar as he spoke, but the doctor stuck to him like glue.

14

"Are you," Saul asked, "one of those heart transplant doctors we have heard so much about?"

"No, not quite. But you're getting warm. You see, my specialty is transplantation of sex organs. Male sex organs to be specific."

"*Sex organs?*" Saul asked, without concealing his surprise.

"Yes, they are really coming into their own of late."

"Sex organs? Haven't they always been popular?"

"No, you misunderstand. I mean *that* type of transplant."

"I see. Go on, go on," Saul urged. His interest rose like a flame in a bale of excelsior. He forgot about Harry. Saul touched the doctor's arm. "Let's go over to the bar for another drink, Doc, and you can tell me all about it."

As they progressed toward the bar, the doctor began to explain: "Let me begin by giving you a little background on just one type of problem that has come to our attention. We refer to it as the 'Penis-minim Problem.' Through our extensive research, my colleagues and I have found that many men are secretly ashamed of the size of the...aah...penis." Although the doctor uttered the last word in a guarded tone, Saul noticed that a white-haired lady in a pink cocktail dress, who had been standing with her back to them at the bar, seemed to stiffen up. As the doctor continued, the woman appeared to be slowly leaning back in their direction, her double-chin tucked into her neck. Saul, more than a trifle embarrassed, started easing the doctor away from the crowded bar. The lady in pink, meanwhile, was still edging backwards towards the pair. Suddenly her escort grabbed her elbow. "My dear, I really think you've had enough! You almost seem to be falling over backwards."

"No, no. I'm fine, George," the woman hastily replied. "Just stretching my back a bit, that's all."

At a safe distance at last, Saul urged the doctor to continue. After taking a quick sip of his martini, the doctor went on: "Well, this Penis-minim condition can, of course, have severe repercussions with respect to a man's marital attitudes. Many men in fact, do not consider themselves fit candidates for marriage because of this problem. Their embarrassment is extreme. Do you know that some men would simply love to go to a health club to exercise but fear they would be laughed at in the shower room because of their tiny organ? A serious psychological problem indeed! Then, there is another group, usually of men approaching middle age or thereabouts, who develop concern that the youthful size of the organ diminishes with passing years. These in the latter group are particularly unfortunate because most of them have been married for many years and have a dreadful fear of losing their wives to younger men."

"All well and good, Doctor, but what about Viagra? Doesn't that help?"

"I'm afraid you don't understand me. It may help performance, but I am mainly talking about *size*, my friend. And don't forget, this has a major impact on satisfaction in the female. By the way, how old are you, Mr. Steinberg?"

Saul laughed. "I'm thirty-eight, but don't look at me, Doc. I'm fine. Fit as a fiddle," he said somewhat dishonestly. He had a sudden urge to reach down just to make sure everything down there was OK, but he decided that under the circumstances, all he could do was jiggle the tab on the zipper of his trousers slightly. "Yes, Doc, fit as a fiddle."

Unheeding, the doctor gave Saul an appraising inspection, apparently looking not so much at the tall trim figure, the dark wavy hair that curved atop the pleasantly good-looking face, but rather searching for the minute tell-tale signs that bubble up to the surface from deep physiological malfunctions. A trace of blue in the lips? Embolisms of the blood vessels in the corners of the eyes? A sallow tone, perhaps, in the skin coloring? Falling hair in the eyebrows? Things that only a doctor can see - much the way a jeweler examines the tiny imperfections in a diamond, while others, untrained in professional rigor, are content to stand back, judging merely by size and sparkle.

The doctor's lip-pursed gaze was so intent on him that Saul, feeling some discomfort, half expected the doctor to conclude by saying: "Be sure to get this prescription filled as soon as possible, and pay the nurse a hundred dollars on your way out."

"Now Doc," Saul continued, as the doctor seemed to straighten up, concluding the brief impromptu examination, "Doc, getting back to what we were saying about this penis stuff, maybe, as you say, some men have problems in that department, but *really* what can you do about it?"

"Transplant!" the doctor responded quickly. "When in doubt, my good man, we *transplant*. Never jeopardize sacred matrimony for a condition that is so easily rectified."

"But exactly *how* is it easily solved? Where the hell do you get the replacement organs?"

"Replacement organs? Let me explain. We have an established group of doctors who are beginning to develop a Sex Organ Bank on a national scale. We are a division of the Organ Transplant Society of America. The acronym is simply OTSA."

"Oh, so you represent what one might call the S.O.B. division of OTSA."

"Precisely. We intend to scour the United States to find donors for the poor unfortunates who suffer this ailment."

"Do you have some kind of donor card that a person fills out when he dies that leaves the organ to the, what is it again? the S.O.B.?"

"Yes. Here's one, now that you asked."

"Gee, thanks."

"But please understand, Mr. Steinberg, we can't use donations after death or at the point of death. We have tried this but it just doesn't work. You see, the male sex organ is very much more delicate than say, kidneys, heart and such like. We have found that donors must be alive and well."

"Now wait a minute!" Saul said challengingly as he crumpled the S.O.B. card in his hand. "I've heard of live donors for kidney transplants; after all, the average person has two, but do you really expect to find anyone willing to donate the only private part he's got?" Saul felt a slight tingling in his trousers. He was tempted again to reach down for reassurance but he resisted it and, having the drink in one hand, merely yanked up and down on his trousers at the belt line with his free hand.

"I didn't say it was *easy* to find donors," the doctor retorted a little sharply.

Saul was incredulous. "Do you think men will accept this?"

"They've accepted vasectomies, haven't they?"

"But this is a whale of a lot different, Doctor."

"Not really," countered the doctor, "not in the strict medical sense. You see, from the medical viewpoint, the protocols are rather comparable: a few snips here and there, and then we go on to closure. And as to the question of donors, for a starter, we are trying to get legislation enacted in the State of Mississippi which would provide for voluntary donations by convicts who could have their sentences reduced thereby."

"You mean *exchanging one sentence for another,*" Saul quipped, pleased with himself.

Harry returned to the patio and walked over to join Saul and the doctor. Harry was fuming. "A dozen closed doors I peek through upstairs. All bedrooms. Not a single toilet in the crowd. Then, ten minutes standing in a long line, only to find they're waiting for autographed pictures of the ambassador and his family."

"So, *where?*" Saul asked.

"Back behind a big tree in the yard," Harry answered in disgust.

Saul shrugged. "Harry, I'd like you to meet Dr. Doctor."

"Let's see now," Harry said puzzled, "your first name is Doctor?"

"No, my first name is John. I *am* a doctor."

"But your last name is...?"

"Yes, that's right," the doctor said with a trace of annoyance, as he turned back to Saul. "Where was I, Mr. Steinberg? Oh yes, and surprising as it may seem there are a number of men in public life who, being workaholics, feel that the sex organ is a handicap to their busy work schedule. And, as I'm sure you know, many a high official has gotten himself in trouble because of his sex organ."

Harry, jerking his thumb towards the doctor, asked Saul: "What's he talking about?"

"I'll explain later," Saul replied.

"And there are other situations," the doctor continued, completely absorbed, and pointedly disregarding Harry. "Now you take a man who gets angry at his wife...and I'm sure you know that some men can get pretty damned angry at their wives. For example, one man called us the other day from somewhere in Iowa...Iowa City, I believe. Wanted us to rush right out with the whole team and do it right on the spot. Under the circumstances, we had to turn him down."

"Why, for heavens sake?" Saul was puzzled. "Since cases like that must be pretty rare, I would think your medical team would grasp at any *thing* they could get their hands on." Saul grinned and poked Harry with his elbow. Harry looked up at Saul quizzically.

The doctor continued in his serious tone. He felt that Saul had raised a critical question, one that should be faced squarely for the good of the society. "Look," he said, "you must realize that we have to exercise caution with this kind of thing. We only want donors who make a calm, rational decision in this regard. We wouldn't want repercussions later. One malpractice suit this early in our program and the S.O.B. would be right out the window."

"Who is the son of a bitch he's talking about?" Harry asked.

"No one, Harry. S.O.B means something else. I'll explain it all to you later."

"And there's another big point in favor of this program," the doctor went on. "You can appreciate, I'm sure, that the S.O.B. can be a dominant factor in dealing with overpopulation."

"But you mean in the case of people *donating* to the bank," Saul interjected, "rather than *receiving*."

Harry, having been left completely out of the conversation, felt he had to say *something*, so, with a self-righteous smile, he proclaimed: "All I can say is that *to give* is more blessed than *to receive*."

"Amen to that," said the doctor. "And now the S.O.B. Division of OTSA is hoping to attract presidential interest in our program. We would have a much better chance of success, both nationally and internationally, if we could get our incoming president involved." The doctor glanced around the patio saying: "I was hoping he would be here tonight. I understand he was invited."

Even though Harry could still not fathom the topic the two men were discussing, at the mention of the president, he said: "Look, Mister Doctor, I don't know what you're trying to do but I know it has something to do with sex and sons of bitches and it sounds a little crazy to me and I wish you would leave my son out of it."

The doctor stiffened. His voice took on an edge. "I said, 'the *president*,' not your son."

"The new president *is* my son," Harry threw back at him, flushed now. "And I think you should leave him alone. Enough problems already my poor David will be facing without having to put up with..."

"Oh, pardon me," exclaimed the doctor. "You must be referring to our new Jewish...aah, I mean our new president-elect, David Fishman. And you must be Harry Fishman, his father. Well, congratulations, Sir. My, my, imagine meeting the father of the new president. How delightful." He turned to Saul: "Are you related to the new president, too?"

"In a way," Saul answered. "I'm a cousin-in-law." Saul was about to explain the blood and marriage chain that remotely tied him to the incoming president, but the doctor had turned back to Harry.

"Now please don't get me wrong, Mr. Fishman," the doctor said. "We're not trying to get your son's private...aah... well, let me put it this way: I am only interested in your son's general support of the program. He might give a few acknowledgments in the Oval Office, a little helping hand. That's all."

The doctor's wife came up and tugged on his sleeve. He introduced her to Saul and Harry. She seemed impressed to meet the president-elect's father. "John, we haven't eaten yet," she said to the doctor. "The buffet is out back."

"Yes, Dear, in a minute. Gentlemen, let's get together and discuss this again sometime. Perhaps over lunch. Mr. Fishman, pleasure to meet you, Sir. Here is my card. And Mr. Steinberg, perhaps you could explain the S.O.B. to the president's father."

Smiling, the doctor shook hands with both of the men and taking his wife by the hand, strolled away.

Harry looked down at the small white card the doctor had slipped into his hand during the handshake. In engraved black letters, it read: Doctor John

Doctor, Director, S.O.B. Division of the Organ Transplant Society of America. Free examination on request.

Harry nudged Saul. "What's this all about? He's got some kind of strange program?"

"Well, Harry, let me explain. You remember the old gag about the gal who chased the guy around the church until she caught him by the organ?"

"Of course. I told it to you."

"Well, this guy wants to go a little further. He and a group of doctors are going around the country collecting male sex organs."

"He sounds like a dirty shmuck," Harry said, shaking his head in contempt.

Saul shrugged. "No, I wouldn't call him a shmuck. He's more of a *shmuck collector.*" But before Saul could launch into the details of the S.O.B., he noticed Harry's wife, Rose, and his wife, Sylvia, beckoning to them from the main reception room.

As the two men joined the ladies, Saul marveled to himself at the likeness between Rose and Harry. They were both short, although average in height for people of their generation, with squat figures and nearly identical silver-gray hair. Someone had commented that after almost fifty years of marriage, what did you expect? The same food, the same ups and downs, watching the same TV shows, couples begin to look more like brother and sister than husband and wife.

"How did you enjoy the party on the back patio?" Harry asked as he and Saul joined the ladies.

"Wonderful!" Sylvia exclaimed. "The buffet there is even better than the one on the side. "Saul, have you eaten anything yet?"

"No, I'm not terribly hungry," Saul replied, downing the last of his martini. "I'll eat later."

"Please, Saul, why should we have to go out later to eat dinner in a restaurant? All you could hope to want is spread out here. So please go and eat."

Saul invited Harry to join him in the buffet line, but Harry refused complaining that an earlier taste of the strange cooking had been enough for him. "Watch out for the meat in the brown gravy, Saul. I don't want to be impolite, so let me just say it has an *unusual* taste."

Rose and Sylvia disagreed, saying the meat was tender and delicious. So, Saul went off alone, through the rooms on the first floor of the mansion, down the back steps, past the orchestra playing on a side stage, and started through the buffet line under the party tent.

So They Went and Elected a Jewish President

Taking a plate, Saul noticed that the man in front of him looked familiar. Then, he realized it was no less than the ambassador himself.

Saul remembered shaking hands with the ambassador in the receiving line just after he and Sylvia had arrived at the party. They had waited outside of the residence for a few minutes before going in because they were supposed to meet Rose and Harry. But seeing no sign of Rose and Harry, they finally decided to go in by themselves.

Then, as Saul and Sylvia had gone through the receiving line, at the announcement, "Mr. and Mrs. Steinberg," the ambassador had not been able to recall any special significance attached to the name Steinberg. Added to that, the press photographers had ignored the couple, so the ambassador gave Saul the usual limp fish handshake, a half-smile and a muttered hello.

Saul recalled that his wife had received a considerably warmer greeting than he, since the ambassador was reported to be an admirer of good-looking, well-proportioned young women. However, they both felt that their first embassy receiving line had been a disillusioning experience, perhaps even a humbling one.

After they had gone through the receiving line, Saul had asked Sylvia where the hell Rose and Harry were. "Remember, we weren't actually invited. Rose and Harry just asked us to come along with them. They said it would be all right. But now they don't show up and we wind up going through that long damn line alone. I really felt like an intruder and a nobody."

"Well, you aren't quite a nobody," Sylvia had retorted. "You're related to the new president, after all. That is, darling, you're related *through me*."

As the evening wore on, Sylvia and Saul had remained alone at the party where they knew absolutely no one, waiting for Rose and Harry, and Sylvia's brother, Hymie and his wife, Shirley.

It was a full hour before Rose and Harry had arrived with apologies for having been caught in traffic and, in fact, by the time they arrived the ambassador's receiving line had been disbanded.

*****

As Saul started filling his plate at the buffet table on the back lawn, the Indonian Ambassador, who had by then downed several martinis, and had had an opportunity to relax and mingle with his guests, was jovially filling his own plate. The ambassador, a short pudgy man with a tanned round face, displayed a mouthful of gleaming white teeth that matched his white jacket. He proudly wore a wide red sash that crossed diagonally down from his

21

shoulder over a huge stomach. A small replica of the blue and gold Indonian shield was fastened to the upper part of the sash.

The ambassador looked over at Saul. "I'll bet you're an American aren't you? Here, have you ever tried any of this? He ladled a large spoonful of meat strips floating in thick brown gravy onto Saul's plate. Saul tasted a bit, thinking, I'll say this for them, they don't monkey around when they cook. Aloud, he said, "This is mighty tasty!"

Saul suddenly stopped, his fork poised in the air as he recalled something he had read about the Indonian Islands. He wondered, but said nothing. Then, smiling along with the ambassador, Saul and the dignitary moved along the buffet table together, sampling here and there. Although the ambassador took pains to describe many of the Indonian delicacies, he never once said anything about the meat. And Saul was afraid to ask especially when he saw half-a-dozen spider monkeys scampering around the lawn. Every now and then a monkey would stop to stare soulfully at the table and emit a low mournful sound.

"Enjoying the party?" the ambassador asked.

"Yes, very much. In fact, this is the first embassy party I've been to."

"Well, from here on you should plan to go to a lot of them; that is, if you are invited. By the way, were you invited to this one or did you just stop in off the street?"

"No, I was invited," Saul replied.

"I see. No harm meant. I was just curious. I understand that a number of Americans just drop by to these parties to take their evening meal and have a few drinks. Well, that's the way it is in free societies. In my country, such offenders would be confined with bread and water for a month."

"Do you want to see my invitation?" Saul asked as he made a show of fumbling through one pocket after another. He looked around on the ground. "It must have fallen out somewhere."

"The ambassador lowered his eyes. His face showed traces of a smirk. "No, no," he protested genially. "That isn't necessary. As I said, I was just mildly curious."

Saul straightened up thinking: When I came in I was kind of treated like a nobody, which maybe I am, but now this shmuck is giving me a hard time. Before he could stop himself, Saul was telling the ambassador that he was related to the new president.

"You are a relative of the incoming president?" exclaimed the ambassador. Dropping his plate on the buffet table, he turned to face Saul. "I don't remember shaking your hand in the receiving line."

"Didn't think you would," Saul replied.

So They Went and Elected a Jewish President

The ambassador grasped Saul's hand, saying with enthusiasm, "Here let me try again." He gave Saul the handshake of his life, complete with a high and wide pumping motion. "Do you get to see the president-elect very often?"

"Oh yes, quite regularly," Saul lied.

"Well, when you see him again, mention that you met me, will you?"

"Oh, of course I will. I'll be happy to tell him."

The ambassador, on tiptoe, scanned the large crowd. "Is there any chance he may be coming here this evening?"

"Probably not. He is very busy you know."

"Tell me Mr...er...aah..."

"Steinberg."

"Yes, Mr. Steinberg. How many relatives would you say the new president has?"

"In all, I'd say several hundred."

"That many?"

"Yes, he comes from a big family."

The ambassador, turning and somewhat ruefully surveying the bone-crushing crowd, asked, "Are they all here at the party?"

"No, there are only four of us here, as far as I know. Many in the family haven't come to Washington yet. After all, he only won the election last month. Takes time to pack and all that."

"You say there are four of you here. Who are the others?"

"My wife, for one. And the president-elect's mother and father are here."

"They are? Where, for heavens sake?"

"Here they come now," Saul answered, spying Rose and Harry strolling in his direction across the back patio, with Sylvia tagging along. "Hey, Harry! Harry Fishman. Come on over. The ambassador wants to say hullo to you."

The ambassador was tickled pink. He called his wife over.
Then, as Harry stepped up to shake hands, the ambassador motioned to the press photographers. However, the photographers merely glanced over, and not seeing anything special about Harry, shrugged and went back to talking in a little knot.

"Take a picture, you idiots," the ambassador demanded in a voice that seethed with a stifled scream. "Take it! Take it!"

By the time the photographers had retrieved their cameras and were set up for the shot, Rose, Sylvia and Saul had moved in closer, standing next to Harry and the ambassador. Next, the ambassador's wife and their three children crowded in. Also squeezing into the group were Sylvia's brother, Hymie, with his wife, Shirley, who had just arrived at the party. As the group grew, the photographers had to move back. One commented that he should have brought a super-wide angle lens. One of the photographers wanted to hold the shot until they could pull off the tiny monkey that had wrapped its arms around Harry's lower pants leg. But the ambassador screamed, "Take the picture! Take it!" So, the picture was taken, but if the new president ever saw the picture in the next day's newspaper, it would have been almost impossible to pick out the ambassador in the mob. There was so much confusion and movement, the only figure that wasn't somewhat blurred was the monkey.

Shortly after, to the loud trumpeting of conch shells, the guests were asked to gather in a large semi-circle on the back lawn for an event that had been promised, and for which they were eagerly awaiting: the Indonian Islands Hupa Show.

As the crowd hushed, to the steady beat of exotic island drums, slowly, from behind a cluster of palm trees came two human streams. Naked young men came around the left side, naked young ladies, from the right. Since both the young men and women wore long black hair bedecked with flowers, the only way the audience could distinguish the sexes came from occasional glimpses of their private parts showing through the folds of cascading hair.

A ripple of applause greeted the entrance of the troupe.

Doctor John Doctor, the transplant surgeon, happened to be standing next to Saul. "Oh, my God," he said in a muted voice, "Do you see what I see?"

"Talk to the ambassador," Saul said with a grin. "Maybe he'll let you take your team down to the Indonian Islands. It would be a gold mine. They might have one of those kings who sees to it that only eunuchs wait on the queen."

The dancers paired off, standing inside hoops that were about three feet in diameter. A young man and a young woman stood facing each other inside each hoop. In all, there were about eight couples.

Saul commented that the hoops looked like plain old hula hoops to him, but the ambassador, standing a few feet away, glanced over and pointed out that they were actually *hupa* hoops dating back five hundred years, and that the Hupa was an ancient Indonian tribal dance. "You know, Mr. Steinberg, you Americans didn't invent *everything*!"

As the drumbeat quickened, the Hupa dance couples began swinging their torsos doing the Hupa in an increasing frenzy of motion, shouting the

24

while: "Hoo-pah, hoo-pah, HOOP! HOOP! Hoo-pah, hoo-pah, HOOP! HOOP!"

Whenever the dancers shouted "HOOP! HOOP!" Sylvia nudged Saul. Her sidelong glance made it plain she thought the hoop-hoop part a bit distasteful because at that point each dancer would reach out grasping for various parts of the body of the other dancer. The dancers being well trained, more often than not succeeded in making contact, but to the casual observer, their arms flashed out and back so quickly that it really wasn't all that obscene.

Later, the Hupa dance was followed by a tumbling act of tiny monkeys which did not come off too well because the monkeys kept stopping to look wistfully at the big bowl of meat in brown gravy on the buffet table.

Finally, a mountain of fireworks was set off—with towering silver fountains that lit up the area like flashing lightning. It proved to be an exciting and very appropriate finale, one evidently intended to provide guests with a miniaturized example of the Indonian Islands' spectacular sunrises.

Just as the semi-circle of guests was breaking up, Saul whispered to Harry: "Harry, tell me something. Could monkey meat be kosher?"

"Why do you ask? Who would eat a monkey?"

"Oh, I dunno. I just wondered."

Harry knitted his brow. "Well, let me see. In Deuteronomy it says that a four-footed animal that possesses a cloven hoof and chews its cud, is an acceptable food. So, we would consider that after blessing by a rabbi, it would be kosher. But..." Harry said, as he glanced down at the tiny monkey that had grabbed him playfully around the lower leg, "a two-legged animal that chews a pants leg, of that I'm not really sure."

4

Alitalia Flight 698 from Rome touched down shortly before seven A.M. in a blinding snowstorm on Dulles runway three-zero and skidded to a stop. The big jet, wingtip and tail beacons flashing, turned off the runway and rolled along the slick concrete apron.

General Ali Karasek peering through a window in the first class cabin, grumbled at the swirling snow. Then, as the hatch opened on the plane, he gave a quick smirk to the flight attendants and wheeled his black carryon bag through the ramp into the terminal. The airplane had been almost empty, confirming his opinion that only a fool or a person with unavoidable business would leave the sunswept Mediterranean to come to Washington in the dead of winter.

As he walked through the terminal to the baggage carousel, he thought of his home in Al Humaydah, Saudi Arabia on the eastern shore of the warm blue Gulf of Aqaba, from whence his journey began. His trip had taken him first to Athens for a brief holiday and then on to Rome for another holiday, and finally to the U.S. He always tried to begin his missions with one or more relaxing holidays. Being a deliberate assassin, he found they put him in a frame of mind in which he could begin methodical planning.

By Allah, how he longed to be handling the wheel of his 600-horse inboard cruiser, the Yamama named after his birthplace at the edge of the great Rub' al Khali Desert in southeastern Saudi Arabia. He could almost feel the heave and roll of the big boat as it plowed across the Aqaba Gulf, the fine, white spray sailing over the windshield and settling on his upturned face. A long roundabout ride, begun shortly before dawn, with four extra fifty-gallon drums of fuel stored below, and culminating in a visit to his friends the Israelis at the military post near the southern tip of the port of Elat. There they would gather in the dark back room of the Intelligence Division, sometimes for an exchange of information, sometimes the passing of money, and on occasion a fiery debate over some crucial point of a plan. But they always capped off their meetings with many jokes about Arabs, still more jokes about Israelis, and later there would be the pleasant, but roundabout ride home.

Karasek did not look like a general. More likely, he resembled a squat, fat, successful businessman. And although he liked the title of general and was permitted to use it, he was retired from the Saudi army. The people who knew him thought of him as jovial and bouncy, although there was a side of him that could grow melancholy to the point of tears. Those who knew him in a professional sense however, recognized him as a clever and meticulous operative, one who could levy the death penalty and execute it himself without thinking twice about it.

After release from Customs in the Dulles Terminal where he used his Israeli passport, he stopped to buy a morning paper. As he pocketed his change, Karasek's eye was caught by a long curved sword embellished with a braided red cord and a gaudy gold tassel— a tourist item hanging in a shop window. The cheap toy sword brought back memories from his childhood. He thought of his father, descended from a line of Bedouins, and the flash of his father's fine steel blade during that last fierce battle on camelback in the desert at Jabrin, near young Ali's birthplace. A young lad then, he had watched the battle from a distance. And he remembered how, shortly after the battle, his father had died a hero's death, or so he thought.

"He died of gall bladder infection with pancreas and liver complications," the doctor had said as he looked up from the bed on which Ali's dead father lay.

In the dark one-room dwelling, lit only by a dim oil lamp, the boy and his mother had stood together in the circle of light as the doctor pressed closed the dust-caked eyelids and pulled the coarse blanket over the head of the newly deceased. As soon as his father's face was covered, in a sudden rage, the ragged ten-year-old boy kicked wildly at the doctor's legs, screaming obscenities at him.

Resh, the parttime village doctor, was startled by the outburst, but quickly understood that the boy, having seen the blood running so freely from one of his father's wounds and having just witnessed the battle, could not believe his father did not die of the wounds.

"You blaspheme him," the boy shouted. "By Allah, he died of the sacred wounds of battle."

The outburst continued until Resh, kneeling down, tried to pin young Ali's flailing arms and legs. The doctor glanced up at the boy's mother and managed a grin despite a flurry of blows on his chest from the small bony fists that pounded like small stones. To Ali, he said, "I agree. Your father died of battle wounds." To Ali's mother, the doctor said, "I like his spirit! When this is over, send him to me and I will make a man of him."

*****

Young Ali's mother was Jewish. On that dark night, a year before Ali was born, who might have thought that a pretty Jewish maiden would have been silently riding alone, deep in the middle of Rub' al Khali desert country, halfway between the Red Sea and the Persian Gulf, so many miles away from

Jerusalem. Her nearly spent Arabian stallion had been intercepted with ease by Ali's father. And just as his father had made the most of the capture and had taken the woman in and kept her as his wife, so too had their loin product, young Ali Moishe Karasek, made the most of his two worlds. Half-Arab, half-Jew, young Ali learned to glean the best of both. He learned early that governments and political factions are eager for information about people's comings and goings and jealously guarded secrets. He soon became aware of special talents he possessed for gathering, analyzing, and later selling such information.

After his father's death, and after his mother galloped off again on horseback into the desert looking for whatever she had been seeking when his father had interrupted her journey eleven years before, young Ali Moishe Karasek was already a fledgling spy. He began selling a few bits of information but was hampered by the fact that he was untrained, and when his only money-contact disappeared, he thought that to be the end of it.

A month after his mother's abrupt departure, Ali, homeless and without money, was spending his days drifting around the town of Yamama stealing bits of food and frequently killing village cats which he roasted in a small cave near the edge of town. As the boy wandered the streets, the Jewish half of him keenly felt the loss of his mother, while the Arab half was jaunty, even happy, that she was gone. This half had never quite reconciled itself to the mother's Semitic ways, and had felt shame at customs that were somehow out of place in Saudi Arabia. Especially unpleasant was the way his mother had kept pushing chicken soup and strange fish dishes. It almost seemed as if she was taking revenge on him, and more particularly on his father, for tying her down in a foreign land.

In this time, his growing years, Ali could not have known that later he would be thankful for his Jewish blood. He did not suspect that this odd chemistry would later open doors, particularly the door to modest fortune.

Resh, meanwhile, going about his rounds as parttime doctor and fulltime thief, frequently came upon young Ali playing in the dusty streets of Yamama. The tall, gaunt, hawk-nosed Resh would lean over waggling a long bony finger at the boy and warn him that a homeless boy, truant from school, would soon be sent away to prison. According to Resh, the townspeople would soon take action, not because they cared a fig about Ali, but because the town was not safe for family pets as long as the hungry boy was on the loose. So, Ali finally went to live with Resh. He was provided with bed, board, a rudimentary education at the local school and a sophisticated education in the art of stealing information. Ali was also free to steal whatever else he could get his hands on in any unguarded tents of the Bedouin tribes that occasionally camped near the village.

Resh, a quiet but resourceful man, had become disillusioned with medicine and for a very good reason. His neighbors' Moslem stoicism in bearing illness and pain even to the point of death, had left him frustrated and penniless. He often said that a village like Yamama did not have any need for a doctor. Resh had learned that remuneration was far better in other fields of endeavor and it was into these 'other' fields that he introduced Ali.

The eager and daring lad became a willing pupil as Resh taught him how to collect information on people of his own and neighboring villages, so that after awhile, young Ali had a dossier on almost everyone in the surrounding area. Into a series of notebooks he carefully transcribed scraps of information. From under a table in a town tavern, or hiding behind a group of resting camels, he recorded even the expressions on people's faces when speaking or reacting to political comments. Nothing escaped Ali's notice or lacked the creative embellishments of his pen.

At that time, two separate governments were attempting to gain control of all of Saudi Arabia: Hejaz in the west at Mecca and Nejd in the east at Riyadh, making an ideal climate for political intrigue. Ali's neatly hand-written dossiers were highly marketable.

The doctor watched with relish as his young student performed spectacular feats of imagery, some of it so beautiful it rivaled Arab poetry. Ali's light, but extremely tasty political soufflés brought as much as 500 to 800 silver riyals when put into the right hands. Of these amounts however, Ali received but a minor share since the doctor insisted on keeping the major portion in return for having provided Ali not only with bed and board, but also for having trained him in the business.

Inevitably, the day came when Ali received the full share: the day when he turned in a dossier on the doctor.

A few years later found Ali expertly handling intelligence in Saudi Arabia for the Jordanians, and in Jordan for the Saudis, after which he would turn over the complete package to his smiling Iraqi contacts for an additional sum. At fifteen, Ali Karasek had become one of the wealthier kids in his part of the world.

At sixteen, Ali had tasted his first virgin, although not his first woman, while on a holiday in Athens; at seventeen, his first kosher hot dog at a deli on West 168th Street. The latter while on a holiday visiting his long lost maternal relatives in the Bronx. At eighteen, Ali had killed his first man while on a holiday in Baghdad in a knife fight over a woman. From all of this he concluded that despite the fondness of his tastes for women and kosher hot dogs, he relished killing best. Holidays *second* best.

*****

As he walked through the Dulles terminal and slipped into the seat of a waiting taxi for the trip to downtown Washington, Ali Karasek was aware that despite the cold and the snow, he was in somewhat of an upbeat mood. There was much to look forward to because he had come to the United States on an extended holiday of sorts and expected to cap this pleasure with the opportunity to kill another man. He would embark on two favorite activities all rolled up in one.

As to the killing, with Karasek up to his usual form, it would be meticulously planned. He was prepared to spend months in preparation, culminating in the few minutes needed to perform the actual deed. And, in keeping with his customary methods, someone else would take the blame. He also had a method for picking the scapegoat. Karasek was one of the few men in the world, possibly the only one, who through his unusual talents and heritage, could be found at a meeting one day with the Israelis and the next, at a meeting with members of one of the Arab countries. In matters of loyalty his principles were simple and universal. They were based completely on money. Karasek frequently found himself on the payroll of "both sides" so he used money as a measure of the direction of swing in the pendulum of his loyalty. And since the Israelis had swung the most for this caper, he would naturally arrange for the Arabs to take the blame. It was unfortunate but necessary.

On that early morning, as the taxi droned along the Dulles airport access road in the direction of Washington, Karasek sank back in the interior of the vehicle and lit a cigarette. He ignored the "No Smoking" sign and the objections of the taxi driver.

Karasek's mind churned over in rhythm with the snow tires that whirred along the hardpacked road. He thought of his task. It was quite straightforward: to kill the incoming U.S. president; and the circumstances quite ideal because he was being paid by both sides to do it. The United States, in the eyes of the Arabs, had just completed the biggest blunder in its history by electing a Jew as president, a Mr. David Fishman. Put simply, the Arabs wanted him dead because *he was a Jew*. Half-Arab himself, Karasek could understand the irrational fear that had led them to this conclusion. But he knew that the Arab reaction was stupid and unrealistic, stemming as it did from centuries old biases. However, he was hardly the one to argue with them on this subject.

So They Went and Elected a Jewish President

A select and powerful group of Israelis also wanted Fishman dead for reasons which at first might seem obscure, but which were far more realistic. In the recently concluded presidential campaign, Fishman had given many assurances of impartiality: a kind of Kennedy-renunciation-of-the-pope in matters involving the United States and Israel. Unbelievably, Fishman had also been quoted as saying he wanted to closely re-examine foreign aid to the Israelis. In some speeches for example, Fishman had almost sounded as if he were *anti*-Israel.

Given the winning presidential slate, one that promised sharp curtailment of U.S arms exports and military intervention overseas only in situations that posed a direct threat to the United States, the Israelis felt they would have been safer if the U.S. had elected a non-Jewish president. In the topsy-turvy world of international politics, such a man, like recent presidents, might have done the opposite of Fishman, bending over backwards to give assurance to U.S. Jews while providing enhanced aid to the Israelis. For Karasek it would always be a game that one managed never to take too seriously. With a wry smile he lowered the window of the taxi and chucked his cigarette butt into the deep snow.

Driving through downtown Washington, Karasek took delight in observing the latest motor cars and sport utility vehicles. Although somewhat obscured by the falling snow, the gleaming colors, tinted windows, luxuriously wide deep-treaded tires, as good in the desert as in the snow, gave him sweet recollection of combat.

He remembered his first command, and still one of his finest hours in battle, as a fledgling major in charge of a motorized regiment. In the Yemen Civil War, the Saudi Arabian government had decided to "lend a helping hand" in the form of sending several Saudi regiments into the fray to help unseat the Yemeni government. In August of '68, in the South Arabian Desert, Karasek in the lead car, drove a headlong charge across the desert through a hail of rifle and machine gun fire, all the while ignoring bazooka and mortar bursts off to the sides. During the charge, Karasek remained standing on the front passenger side of the open convertible, his left hand gripping the top molding of the windshield, his right cutting holes in the air with his father's glittering curved sword. Occasionally, he would fire his pearl-handled pistol in the air in a kind of Pattonesque symbol that spurred on his small army.

Under the hot desert sun, the lead car, a bright red Chevrolet Impala convertible, varoomed along the flat, hardpacked desert floor, followed by a formation of almost fifty bright orange Chevy Malibu 4-door sedans that had their roofs sawed off, six men to a car, rifles jutting menacingly skyward.

31

Since Karasek had ordered that all the mufflers be taken off the cars, the roar was deafening.

Karasek's regiment completely routed a much larger force of the enemy whose camels became about as nervous as pedestrians trying to cross the street in midday Manhattan.

It became clear from this battle that in the lands bordering the Red Sea, the Arabian Gulf and the Persian Gulf, the cantankerous camel had seen the end of his days in desert warfare. Karasek later conceded that most of the plaudits were rightly due to the Chevrolet Division of General Motors in Detroit and a little-known used car dealer in Beirut from whom Karasek had purchased the cars, later armoring and painting them, and teaching his men how to scare the entrails out of camels with them.

In the battle of '82, after which Karasek was promoted to the rank of general, his updated force of sturdy Volvos drove rings around a much larger force of enemy Volkswagens. Although highly maneuverable, the beetles had not been able to stand up to the battering head-on collisions. After the battle, the desert was littered with overturned Volkswagens, bumpers, fenders and miscellaneous automotive debris. Again, the real credit went to the automobile manufacturer according to Karasek; and although a few of his men had suffered superficial gunshot wounds, the only serious injuries were to the improvident few who had neglected to fasten their seat belts.

The taxi carrying General Karasek pulled up in front of the Continental Hotel, situated at the edge of Union Station Plaza and within view of the United States Capitol Building. The general trudged through the snow. Inside, he walked to the front desk, checked in under the name, Moishe Silverman, and had his bags taken up to his room. Next, he made a few telephone calls from the pay booth in the hotel lobby, and then went into the coffee shop to have a late breakfast and read his American newspaper.

Through it all, Ali Karasek had one principal concern. He knew he could not do the job alone; he would need several fellow agents, and he wondered who the Arab countries would send to be part of his team.

5

On the morning following the Indonian ambassador's party, Sylvia sat up in bed and reached over to shake Saul who was still asleep next to her. Getting no response, she hopped out of bed, slipped into her robe and hurried to the window of the hotel room to view the city from the vantage point of the eighth floor. "Not a single skyscraper," she mumbled half aloud. It sounded like a criticism, but it wasn't. Sylvia's heart was filled with happy excitement. She loved Washington. No giant skyscrapers here. None of the so called 'canyons of steel.' A far more relaxed atmosphere than in her hometown, New York, and, all in all, a nice collection of plump white federal buildings.

"What does it look like?" Saul asked sleepily, propped on one elbow in bed and trying to focus his eyes against the stark whiteness flooding into the room through the large picture window.

"You *know* what it looks like, dear. We've been down here before."

"Yes, but describe it anyway. Maybe it has a different flavor now that we're going to call this town home."

"Well, let me see. It looks like Rome, circa one hundred A.D., except for the cars and the snow."

Saul, groaning at the thought of having to drive in the snow that day to hunt for an apartment, pulled a pillow over his head. A muffled voice came from beneath the pillow: "How could there be snow? It was sixty-five degrees yesterday! I know because we were at the Indonian ambassador's party. We were outside on a balmy evening. No coats. Don't you remember that those Hupa dancers didn't look cold and they were naked."

"I remember. I remember! But it must have started snowing after we got back to the hotel. Looks like a foot at least out there."

Saul went to the window. He took a quick look then wrapped his arms around his wife. He could feel her warm soft body underneath her robe. A few moments later, Saul was on top of her trying to make love to her on the floor.

Sylvia wriggled out of her robe to spur him on but then playfully rolled from one side to the other, constantly fending him off. She put up a pretty fair battle. She wanted him to appreciate it when he got it by making him struggle for it...and he always did. Sylvia also liked the way sex strengthened the muscles surrounding her spinal column. After eight years of marriage to Saul, she had developed a strong and flexible back.

Saul, although always eager at first, with a libido as powerful as a starving dieter reaching for a candy bar, nevertheless seemed to have trouble performing, petering out halfway through their lovemaking. She thought he might be upset over money and job difficulties. "What's the matter, Saul?"

"I dunno. Maybe I'm just tired."

"Shouldn't you go see a doctor? He might give you a prescription for Viagra. Maybe that would help."

"My god, age thirty-eight and already my future happiness depends on a bottle with little blue pills inside!"

*****

Sylvia and Saul slipped into a booth in the Continental Hotel coffee shop. The partly frosted window beside them was speckled with snowflakes, while outside, the adjacent street held a glut of morning rush hour traffic stalled in the snow. Peering through the window, they could dimly see the outline of the U.S. Capitol Building almost hidden behind a thick wall of falling snow.

They ordered breakfast and then sat in silence, enjoying the snug warmth of the shop, and occasionally peering through the window at the frosted world outside.

Sylvia played with her spoon. She glanced over at Saul, her blue eyes suddenly sparkling. "Don't you absolutely love snow?"

"From this side of the window, yes."

Her expression clouded. "Does that mean you don't want to hunt for an apartment today?"

He dodged the question. "What I'd like to do is chase you around under a blanket."

"Once a day is enough. Remember, you're not as young as you once were."

Sylvia realized that despite the heavy snow, they really *had* to begin looking for an apartment right away. She was concerned about the cost of the visit to Washington and was anxious to move down and get settled. She knew that Saul felt the same, although he obviously didn't relish the idea of driving all over town in a city that always seemed to be unprepared for, and unable to cope with, snow.

At a table located just across the aisle from where Sylvia and Saul were sitting, a man sat with his face buried in a newspaper. He held the paper spread in the air in front of his face. The couple occasionally had a glimpse of the man's face whenever he lowered the paper for a moment to sip his coffee.

At one point, the man began peering levelly over the top edge of the newspaper. He appeared to be covertly studying Sylvia. His gaze became so intense, she began feeling uncomfortable. She was at the point of making a comment about the man to Saul when the man's gaze suddenly shifted to Saul. Now it was Saul's turn to wonder.

So They Went and Elected a Jewish President

The man cleared his throat. "Pardon me," he said aloud in a pleasant sounding voice that held a trace of a foreign accent, "but I am looking at a picture here in the newspaper that was taken at an embassy party yesterday. It is a bit blurry, but I believe that you two are in the picture. Could that be?" The man rose from his seat and brought the paper to the booth.

At first, Sylvia was slightly wary of the intrusion and doubtful about the picture, but after she had a look at it, her face lit up in surprise. She showed it to her husband. "Look Saul, the picture we had taken with the ambassador. It's in the paper!"

Saul's eyebrows went up as he leaned over for a closer look. Then he looked up at the stranger and asked if he would like to join them. As the man slipped into the booth beside Saul, he smiled politely. "I do not want to seem forward, but may I comment that you are every bit as attractive in person as in the photograph."

Saul was pleased. "Thank you."

"Oh! I did not mean you, I was referring to the lovely lady here."

Sylvia basked in the compliment and Saul was pleased, nonetheless. "Where are you from?" he asked.

"I am just in from Rome. Actually it was only the last leg of my journey. My trip began in the Middle East."

"Quite a ways off. Where in the Middle East?"

"Just a small town. The name would not mean anything to you. By the way," the man said, twisting around to shake hands with Saul, "my name is Moishe; I am here on a holiday."

"With a name like Moishe, you must be Jewish. Are you from Israel?"

"Yes and no."

Saul wondered at the answer, but he didn't say anything.

"You picked an awful season for a holiday in Washington," Sylvia commented, pointing over at the window.

"Yes, so it would seem."

Sylvia was reading the caption under the news photo. She apologized for having practically snatched the man's paper away.

"Quite all right. I was just about all the way through it anyway. In fact, you can clip out the picture if you like, Mrs. Steinbottom."

Sylvia corrected him: "No, our name is Steinberg."

Saul frowned and looked at the paper. He suddenly realized why the man had their name wrong. The paper listed them as 'Mr. and Mrs. Steinbottom from Bensonberg, New York.'

"Well, that sometimes happens," Ali Karasek replied genially. "Incidentally, who are the others in the picture?"

35

Sylvia pointed out two smiling faces in the photograph. "Their names are missing in the caption, but I can tell you they are my aunt, Rose and my uncle, Harry. By the way, they're the parents of the incoming president, David Fishman."

"Oh, then you must be..."

"That's right. He's my cousin," Sylvia said, beaming with pride.

General Karasek looked inquiringly at Saul.

"I'm whatever she is. Just add the word 'in-law.'"

Karasek then pointed to the photo again. "Who are the people at the end of the line?"

"The man with the big cigar?" asked Sylvia. "That's my brother, Hymie. And standing next to him with the big plate of food is his wife. Shirley is going on a diet."

Karasek studied the picture of Shirley. "A diet? What a pity! Why she is absolutely beautiful just as she is."

Sylvia gulped, almost spilling her coffee. A quick glance at the stranger told her he was sincere. She recalled him saying that she, Sylvia, was lovely. But he thinks Shirley is *absolutely beautiful*. I suppose, Sylvia said to herself, there's no accounting for Middle East tastes.

Karasek asked the waitress to bring them another round of coffee. He was in no hurry to do anything that morning, and was delighted over the stroke of good fortune that put him in contact with some of Fishman's relatives. He loved serendipitous coincidences. They were gifts either from Allah or Jehovah. Since he was half and half, he was never sure which.

"Well, this is pleasant running into relatives of the incoming president. I suppose you must be very excited about it all. But tell me now...I do not mean to be offensive...I am as I said, from another country, but what I wonder is how a Jew can be elected president of *this* country. After all, from what I hear, you have only two Jewish cities in the United States: New York and Miami."

"Now wait a minute," Sylvia protested, "there are Jews all over this country." Then, as an afterthought, she added, "And Mr. Fishman is obviously very popular with non-Jews as well. In fact, he never could have been elected on just a Jewish vote, we are a tiny minority."

"True, but I expect you are a pretty solid bloc who fought extra hard for this election."

Sylvia found herself on the defensive. She was getting more and more upset over the direction the conversation had taken. She wondered, Who is this guy? His name is Moishe, but he sounds more like an anti-Semite.

Karasek, noting Sylvia's growing displeasure, looked her straight in the eye. "May I speak plainly?"

"Please do. This is a free country."

"Good. I may sound anti-Semitic, but I am not. That could never be because if I insult a Jew, my right hand insults my left; and if I insult an Arab, my left hand insults my right." He reached for the small plastic container of cream next to his coffee cup. "I am, like what you Americans stir into your coffee: Half and Half."

Saul chimed in. "My, that's an interesting combination. How do you stay alive in the Middle East?"

Karasek glanced at him with a slight grin on his face. "It takes a bit of skill."

"Call for Mr. Silverman, Mr. Moishe Silverman."

"I am Mr. Silverman," Karasek said to the bellhop who was walking through the shop with the message.

"The call is on the phone in the lobby next to the check-in desk."

"Thank you," Karasek said as he pressed a five dollar bill into the bellhop's hand. To Sylvia and Saul, he added, "Please excuse me. This will only take a minute. I will be right back."

After Karasek left, Sylvia grabbed her purse. "Let's go. I've had it with this jerk."

"I haven't finished my coffee. Let's just hang on for a few more minutes."

When Karasek returned, he slipped into the booth next to Saul and looked directly at Sylvia. "As I was saying, Mrs. Steinberg, Fishman...any Jew...as your American president, makes for simply a bad situation. As a Jew, the Arabs find him offensive, and yet the U.S. badly needs Arab oil. He can get the oil, of course, but it would require many concessions and these will tend to alienate Israel. I am sorry, but I think the people of this country have managed to put themselves into...what do you Americans call it? Oh, yes, between a stone and a firm place."

"We call it 'a rock and a hard place,'" Saul said with a grin.

"Oh sorry. My English is not perfect."

Sylvia pointed her finger at Karasek. "All you think of is the Middle East. Mister, it's a big world out there. And oil is available in a lot of other places. On top of that, there are substitutes for oil. And there is something else you're overlooking," Sylvia said, her tone stiffening by the minute. "A Jewish president will make this country number one in trade again. He knows how to improve productivity, create jobs, beef up the economy. In fact, a capitalistic

37

country *without* a Jewish president is like having one of your best athletes sitting on the bench during the Superbowl."

The argument, for such it had become, raged on for another quarter hour. Finally, Sylvia motioned to Saul as she picked up her purse and slipped out of the booth. She stood looking down at Karasek. "And, when you consider how competitive the world has become, I'm surprised how long this country has lasted without having a Jewish president once in awhile."

As they left the coffee shop, Karasek remained behind. In the lobby, Sylvia muttered to Saul: "He seemed, at first, like a friendly old goat, but he certainly got obnoxious fast. He may be half Jew, but he sure came across as two-thirds Arab and one-third obnoxious.

On the way through the lobby, Saul purchased ten copies of the newspaper that had their picture in it. Sylvia purchased six more.

As they waited for the elevator, Sylvia looked at Saul: "What about the restaurant check? I didn't see you pay it."

Saul smiled. "I guess you didn't hear him say he'd pay for it, so I didn't argue with him."

"Good," Sylvia replied, as they both stepped into the elevator. "You're wasting your breath arguing with that kind."

*****

Later in the morning, Sylvia and Saul, huddled in the cold interior of their aging auto, skidded and fishtailed through almost a foot of unplowed snow along Pennsylvania Avenue.

"There's one nice thing," Sylvia volunteered brightly in a loud voice intended to cheer up her husband, "although it doesn't run too well, our old car looks as good as anyone else's when it's covered with all this snow."

Stopped at a traffic light, Sylvia noticed that a pickup truck stopped directly in front of them with all the snow cleared off, had a bumper sticker reading, *DOWN WITH FISHMAN*. Sylvia seethed. "What's the matter with some of the people in this country? They're against everything. He isn't even *up yet*, and already they're saying '*down with*'."

But when Sylvia saw another sign, this one hand-lettered in the rear window of the same truck, her eyes flashed angrily. The hand-lettered sign read: *KEEP THE WHITE HOUSE KOSHER – GET RID OF FISHMAN.*

"What do you mean 'bump into him?'" Saul protested. "You've got to be kidding."

A few blocks further on, at Sylvia's urging, Saul was riding abreast of the truck. She rolled down the window on her side, and through the white swirls gave the other driver a sultry smile and a big wink, all the while running her tongue around her lips like someone ready and willing for a romp in the hay.

When the pickup truck driver spotted the pretty brunette with long fluffy brown hair and bright eyes who seemed of a sudden to be smitten by his profile, he rolled his driver side window full open and craned his neck around to get a better look. In the swirling snow, he apparently did not see her husband driving the car.

At this point, Sylvia held a small folded piece of paper out the window and as the truck driver reached for it, she purposefully let it fall short, landing in the snow between the vehicles. The truck driver abruptly slowed down as Sylvia rolled her window up.

Then, as Saul drove on, in the side rearview mirror, Sylvia saw the pickup swerve, skid sideways and bump up onto the curb.

As Sylvia sat, thoroughly engrossed in filing her nails, it was the first time in her life that she realized how potent a political weapon a pretty face could be. And all along, she had thought it was only good for magazine covers and selling beauty products. And getting married, of course.

"By the way, where are we going?" she asked.

Saul glanced at his wife. "We're looking for an apartment."

"That much I know. What I wanted to know is *where*?"

"Oh. Over in Southeast Washington. The newspaper listed all kinds of apartments to rent over there."

With that, Sylvia laid her head back against the seat headrest. She closed her eyes. As Saul drove, he stole a glimpse at his wife. She was, at thirty-two, a very attractive woman, better looking than when he had married her. He liked her dark brown hair and the way she wore the fluffy curl down on the side of her forehead. The same fluffy curl that had creamed the driver of the pickup truck.

With her eyes closed, Sylvia showed faint traces of a Jewish profile, but when the deep blue eyes were open, she was often mistaken for Irish.

Lying back, eyes closed, but not asleep, Sylvia had a comfortable feeling that at last, things were looking up. Soon, her cousin, David, would be in office, and soon, her handsome husband and she would be smack dab in the middle of an elite social circle. And very soon they would be living in Washington, hopefully close to Rose and Harry, which might improve their chances of being in on things.

Sylvia and Saul had been living in a small apartment in Bensonhurst, New York. It was all they could afford. The ups and downs of Saul's jobs having brought them close to the brink of welfare on more than one occasion.

But lately, Sylvia noticed that her husband had stopped griping about his job at the New Guard Life Insurance Company, so she supposed he was doing better there. After two years, maybe, just maybe, he might make a go of it in the insurance business. His initial commissions had been quite good, although he had been selling entirely to family members and friends and it remained to be seen whether he could cold-sell to strangers. Sylvia was counting on it now that David was the incoming president. She got goose pimples imagining the insurance contacts one could make with a relative in the White House. The old fifty-dollar commissions are dead, so bury them. Alevasholem! And all you rich guys who can afford policies with commissions of five thousand and up: Sholom!

Sylvia smiled, opened her eyes and leaning over, gave her husband a kiss on the cheek.

"What was that for?"

"Oh, nothing. I love you, that's all."

*****

Checking places in Southeast Washington, Sylvia and Saul found many high rise apartments, but all came with high rent, neighborhoods with high crime, streets with high traffic, high noise and high pollution levels. One thing for sure, whatever it was in Southeast, it was high.

"Do Rose and Harry live in this neighborhood?" she asked.

"No, they live on the other side of town in an area called Chevy Chase, just over the D.C. line in Maryland. But Harry told me the rent is so high he has to take a shot of whiskey on the first of the month to get up the courage to write the rent check. And in case you don't think that's high rent, remember, Harry hates the sight of whiskey."

As Saul continued driving, Sylvia, trying to be helpful, suggested that high rent might not be a problem for them now, considering the new insurance contacts Saul could make in Washington. Sylvia, keenly imaginative, could almost see her husband seated at an insurance desk in a back office in the West Wing of the White House. She could almost hear him on the phone talking to New Guard Life field desks he had set up at State, Treasury, the FBI, whatever. Why, he might even start his own insurance company! Endless possibilities presented themselves. But Sylvia was quick to realize it was only a pipedream. David Fishman, she knew, recoiled at even the suggestion of nepotism.

After suggesting they look for an apartment over in Chevy Chase, close to Rose and Harry, and which would be close to the New Guard Life

So They Went and Elected a Jewish President

Insurance headquarters in Northwest Washington, Sylvia heard no response from Saul. A sudden fear gripped Sylvia's heart. She twisted on the seat to stare at her husband. "You're still a New Guard Life Insurance agent, aren't you?"

Again, no answer from Saul, but by then she didn't need one because she already knew the answer from the glum look on his face and the way he sullenly stared at the snow-covered street ahead. Sylvia sat back in the seat. She gazed silently through the window on her side. He had lost another job! She was too dumbstruck to say anything. Her cousin would come to Washington in triumph to take up his position at the White House, while her husband would be at the unemployment office or getting a handout at a welfare office. At that point, if Sylvia moved anywhere, she wanted it to be far away, preferably to a small town in Central America.

Saul finally offered an explanation. He hadn't really lost his job. While he was still 'on the books' as a New Guard agent, it had become somewhat of a technicality. The last time a relative had bought a policy from him was a few months before, and it had been almost a year since a friend had bought one. Now he had no more relatives or friends who were interested, and in numerous attempts, he had found he was incapable of closing a deal with strangers. His boss at New Guard Life was threatening to turn his commission book over to someone else, and on top of that, his residual commissions were so small, they were almost an insult. To say the least, he was upset by the recent turn of events. He felt like sending a note that his New Guard Life boss should drop dead. And when the jerk did, he fondly hoped he didn't have a dime's worth of life insurance!

Sylvia stared out the window. She had learned that arguing with him about jobs and in particular, about lost jobs, did absolutely no good. Her mind raced. In the eight years since she and Saul were married, almost every girlfriend or acquaintance she had, or had even heard about, seemed to marry an industrious sweat-of-the-underchin man. How did she miss the boat? She thought back to the time when they first met. Her initial reaction was that he was handsome. She realized *that* as her first mistake. He had a rugged masculine quality and they got along perfectly, right from the start. He had a college degree in a field for which there was no job market. He was laid back and easygoing. Mistakes piled upon mistakes.

When it came to making money, Sylvia knew she was handicapped. Largely, it stemmed from the fact of her old-fashioned upbringing. Her family had a strict tradition that a Jewish wife should be, first and foremost, a mother and homemaker. Then, with a little time left over, she might get some work on the side. She and Saul had been trying almost every day for eight years to

41

make her a mother, but nothing ever happened. They even started on the first night they were married, for heaven's sake!

The adoption waiting list for a Jewish baby at the agency near them in Bensonhurst was cut off at one hundred couples. If the line was any longer, by the time those at the end of the line had a chance to adopt, they would be too old to care for the baby. The woman at the agency chuckled when she told Sylvia: "Can you imagine an elderly couple taking an adopted baby into a nursing home?"

So through the years, Sylvia had worked only at parttime jobs and did volunteer work for the Red Cross. Then, when her cousin, David, began his campaign, she started working fulltime as a volunteer at his campaign headquarters on Long Island.

"Saul, if you haven't been getting anything much in the way of commissions from New Guard Life, how have we been living?"

"My mother's money. The money she left us when she died. Aleha Ha Shalom."

"How is it holding out?"

"We'll have the expense of moving down here to a new place, buying some new furniture and, all in all, dear, I'm afraid the money is running out of the bottle like the cheap brand of ketchup."

"Are we broke?"

"Hell no! Is a ketchup bottle ever really empty?"

Sylvia let out a sigh that sounded more like a moan.

"But hold on now," Saul said. "I have lots of good ideas. I've been toying with new business ideas."

"How about just looking in the paper and applying for a job?"

"Now, Sylvia, you know that's not my style."

"So, give me some of these 'ideas.'"

"I'd rather not disclose any right now, but I'm thinking that with Harry's help, I could get something big started."

"You mean, Harry's money."

"Yes, some of that, but also his influence with David."

"Oh no," Sylvia said sternly, "you're not going to propose any crazy business ideas to the president. However, if Harry, who has been a businessman all his life and a successful one at that, is willing to give you some help getting started in a sensible venture, I suppose that would be OK."

6

"Mr. Fishman, could I ask you to sit up a smidgeon straighter in the chair?

"Sure. Why not?" Agreeably, Harry wriggled his fanny back against the upright cushion of the brown leather chair. "How's this?"

"That's fine. Hold that pose for a minute, please." The director, standing in the control room, gazed through the glass wall at Harry who was seated in the studio surrounded by an array of lights and TV cameras. The director studied his subject in the monitor. He nodded thoughtfully, the knuckle of his curled index finger pressed into the dimple of his chin. In the monitor he could see Harry seated in the armchair directly in front of an artificial window through which a large color photograph of the White House was visible. On screen, the white-haired Harry, dressed in a dark, well-tailored business suit, appeared to be seated proudly within shouting distance of what would soon be his son's official residence.

When camera two switched on, the director frowned. His voice resounded loudly over the public address system in the studio. "Mr. Fishman, don't you see the red light?"

Belatedly, Harry, blinking under the brilliant lights, looked over to the other camera.

"That's it. Don't you remember what I told you before?" the director asked, his voice taking on a slightly petulant tone. "When the light goes on, on top of the other camera, you're supposed to look over toward it."

Harry raised his bushy white eyebrows. "What's the matter, my profile you don't like?"

"It isn't that, Mr. Fishman; it's just that you're going to be talking to the people through the camera and it's better if you look directly at them."

"All right. I'm looking. So what now?"

"That's fine. But now, could you hold the bottle a bit higher and glance over at it occasionally as you talk, and this time could you do it with a little more......aah......*love* in your expression?"

"But I don't love it," Harry complained looking at the bottle with a slight grimace. "In fact, it's not the kind of soft drink I usually buy. IN FACT, White House brand Banana Carrot Cola I never even knew existed until a few days ago when you called me up. When I had my lunch counter on Long Island..."

"Please, Mr. Fishman, you're being discourteous to our sponsor sitting in the back of the studio."

Harry apologized. He had been dimly aware of a group of people gathered behind the wall of lights and cameras, but was surprised to hear the sponsor was in the audience.

"Now, can we take it from the top, Mr. Fishman? Remember, you start out by saying, 'We in the Fishman family drink White House brand Banana Carrot Cola just about every day.'"

"We-in-the-Fishman-family-drink-White-House-Banana-Carrot- Cola-just-about-every-day." Harry's voice was flat, methodical.

The director shook his head slowly. "Mr. Fishman, that didn't sound very convincing."

Harry shrugged. "I'm not a convincing liar."

A loud HARRUMPH! boomed at Harry from the gloom in the rear of the studio.

Harry, suddenly irritated, HARRUMPHED back. After all, it wasn't easy sitting under the hot lights, with the dazzling glare in his eyes, and having to remember so many little details, and having to sit for such a long period in a stiff position. Harry scowled at the bottle he was holding.

"Mr. Fishman, now you're actually scowling at it!" the director cried out in shock. He ran his fingers nervously through his hair. Then he had an idea. He rapped on the glass partition. "Tell you what, will someone out there bring Mr. Fishman a tall cool glass of the delicious cola?"

When the drink arrived, Harry took a sip. "It tastes interesting," he commented, trying to say what he could about the drink, although he was uncertain about the flavor. Was it a fruit drink or a vegetable drink? He was also wary of the gassy tingle in his throat. "It tastes a little like banana cola and a little like carrot juice."

"Yes, that's the general idea. It's healthy. You get your fruits and vegetables in one drink."

"But I'm still not sure I would actually…...."

The director struggled to remain patient. He thought of another tack. "Mr. Fishman, why don't you sit there, and while you're saying the words on the prompter, try to concentrate, and I mean *concentrate hard* on all the money we're paying you for this commercial. Would that help?"

Harry concentrated hard for a full minute; then, reaching again for the bottle, he bestowed a kiss on it. He held it up next to his face, lavished a broad warm smile on it, and read the words on the prompter with almost the same conviction he had when reading the Bible.

The director smiled. The sponsor smiled, and they made the tape.

*****

So They Went and Elected a Jewish President

Before the commercial was aired, it was brought to the attention of Roger Halstead who was inching closer every day to appointment as the new White House Chief of Staff. Mr. Halstead was not amused. Expatriate British royalty might appear in television commercials without royal backlash, but it was unthinkable for the parent of an American president to become a pitchman for a soft drink. Or anything else, for that matter. When Halstead threatened to alert the auditing division of the Internal Revenue Service, the networks became convinced that it would be too costly to run the tape.

For his effort, Harry received a modest one-time payment. There would be no residuals.

Sylvia loved the apartment and she loved the location, downtown Silver Spring, Maryland, just a thirty minute drive north of the White House. How convenient it would be for David Fishman to visit them, or for them to visit him at the White House after he was sworn in as president. Saul loved the location too. It was only a four-block walk to the nearest synagogue, and better yet, a two-block walk to the nearest Jewish deli. Saul also loved the apartment and its amenities. He especially liked the fitness center located in the basement which was complete with an exercise room, indoor swimming pool and sauna. But on the downside, he thought the elevators were dangerous in the sense that the higher you took the elevator, the higher the rent. Above the tenth floor where Sylvia and Saul settled on an apartment, the rents which were high by any standard, could only be squeezed into the budget of someone who had just won the lottery.

Saul had only one real concern. Soundproofing in new apartments like this one seemed to be sorely lacking. He and Sylvia were having breakfast in the kitchen one morning when Sylvia sneezed. They looked at one another in surprise when the woman in the next apartment said, "Gesundheit." And one afternoon when Saul commented to Sylvia that he thought the matzo-ball soup in the deli was delicious, he thought he heard the woman in the next apartment say, "Yes, but stay away from the knishes, they're too greasy."

From then on, Sylvia and Saul spoke in whispers while eating. But despite all, they really liked the apartment. Although the rent was more than they wanted to pay and more than they could afford, Sylvia and Saul felt they needed a suitable place in the event that David Fishman might drop by. They had no assurance that he would however, since the last time he dropped by was right after they were married eight years before.

There are people who wait for deserts to turn lush green and others who wait for polar ice caps to melt. Sylvia and Saul Steinberg, and especially Sylvia, would wait for the president of the United States to drop by for a cup of coffee and a slice of danish at the end of a tiring day at the White House.

*****

A day after Sylvia and Saul moved into the apartment and no more than twenty minutes after they had a working phone, they received a long distance call from Sylvia's mother in New York. Sylvia answered. "Hello. Who's calling?"

"Who else? This is your mother."

"Momma, how nice to hear your voice, but tell me, our phone was just put in; how did you get the number so quickly?"

"Saul is an expert at losing jobs; I am an expert at finding new phone numbers. When I got your number I was told it was in Silver Spring. I thought you and Saul were moving to Washington. Don't tell me he missed the turn-off and you wound up in Silver Spring, Florida? I always thought Saul was a very nice man; very handsome; some would even call him a mensh, but I am withholding judgment on that. I am not convinced he is highly motivated, and he's certainly not good on directions, and now I'm certain of it."

"Momma, if you keep saying bad things about my husband, I'm going to hang up."

"OK, he's a mensh. Yes, even a shlemiel is sometimes a mensh. Is that good enough?"

"For the moment, maybe. Now, Momma, we're actually in Washington. Silver Spring is a suburb of Washington. We just finished moving into our nice new apartment."

"Do they have a silver spring there, just like Florida?"

"Well, they do and they don't. They have a silver spring, only it's covered up now and it's just a storm sewer, and all things considered, I guess it really isn't silver any more."

"How nice. How is Saul? Is he working?"

"He's fine, Momma. And good news..."

"You're pregnant! Is it a boy? You have to name him Matthew after your father."

"No, Momma, I'm not pregnant. The good news is that Saul is starting a new business. Did you want to talk to him?"

"No. Oh, all right. Let me say hello to him."

Sylvia heaved a deep sigh and with a wry smile, handed the phone to Saul.

"Hello, Momma Fishman. How are you?" Saul tried to smile into the receiver hoping that a little charm might win a few points in a ballgame with his mother-in-law that he had been consistently losing for eight years.

"Hello down there. Sylvia says you missed the turn-off and wound up in Silver Spring, Maryland instead of Silver Spring, Florida."

"Huh?"

"Sylvia says you're living in a nice apartment."

"Yes, Momma. It's quite nice. It's..."

"Oy gevalt! What was that? Do you have a phone in the bathroom? I heard a toilet flushing."

"No, Momma, it was just the toilet in the next apartment."

"You're telling me that when your neighbors go to the bathroom in Silver Spring, I can hear them all the way up here in New York? What kind of a dump are you making my Sylvia live in now?"

"Momma," Saul pleaded, "it's really a very nice place. A new high rise with elevators. Our apartment even has a balcony. We have air conditioning and everything, including very thin walls."

"Oy-oy-oy! What was that? Has Sylvia been fixing you Brussels sprouts again? I keep telling her they're like little gas bombs. Why doesn't anybody listen to me?"

Saul groaned. "Momma, please overlook the sounds. Our phone is right next to their bathroom. Let's just go on with the conversation, can we?"

"Sylvia says you're starting a business. How do you start a business without money? How do you rent the store, buy a cash register, buy the stock, advertise...all without money?"

"It's not a store. I'm going to make movies. I will borrow a camera and what equipment I need and off I go."

"What about people? Don't you need to pay actors? Wait a minute, is this one of those adult movies where you don't even need a wardrobe budget? All you need is a bed and a couple of sex fiends?"

"No, of course not! I'm going into serious moviemaking."

"Could you be more specific?"

"No, Momma, I can't. Like I said, I'm just getting started."

"Just give me a hint. I promise I won't tell anyone about the plot and especially not about the ending."

"Well, if you insist. The story I'm thinking about takes place along the Potomac River. General Robert E. Lee is trying to cross to escape the Union Army."

"You're remaking *Gone With The Wind*!"

"Yes, Momma Fishman, *Gone With The Wind,* only I may give it a new title."

"It's about time someone brought that oldie up to date. It must be fifty-years old! But you'll never find another Rhett Butler like Clark Gable. Such a closing line! 'Frankly, Scarlett, I don't give a damn!' I was shocked like everyone else. But what a movie! I filled a handkerchief by the time it was over."

"Momma Fishman, talk to Sylvia again," Saul said as he handed the receiver to his wife and marched into the living room.

"Hello, Momma, this is Sylvia again. Tell me, are you and Poppa planning to come down for David's inauguration? If you do, you can stay with us in the spare room."

So They Went and Elected a Jewish President

"I have my doubts. My broken hip, although mending well, is still very weak. I can't walk far. And your Poppa hasn't been feeling well lately, and he hates Washington, although he might like a place that has a nice silver spring. Before I sign off Sylvia, there are a few important things I have to say. When you see David, tell him that Poppa and I watch him on TV all the time. Poppa says he is not standing up very straight in front of the cameras, and he should hold his head a little higher. And I think, now that he's elected, it's safe for him to let his hair grow out gray on the temples like it was before. After all, with such an important job, he shouldn't have to worry about a rinse every week. Tell David that when you see him, will you?"

"I'll try, Momma."

"And Sylvia, promise me one thing? Before I hang up, please promise me you'll keep Saul away from Brussels sprouts? This is your mother signing off."

Sylvia walked into the living room and slumped down into an armchair facing Saul. They sat, staring silently at one another for a long time.

"Saul, did I hear you say you're going to do a remake of *Gone With The Wind*? It takes more than a camera and some borrowed equipment to do that."

"It was just an idea off the top of the head. It's only one of the things I'm considering."

"OK, but watch out. Right now I bet Momma's up there telling everyone we know that you are remaking one of the greatest films of all time."

"Well, so what? If I don't do it, I'll simply tell her I changed my mind. By the way, I heard you on the phone inviting them down to stay with us."

Sylvia, shrugging her shoulders, managed a sly smile. "I love them dearly but Momma and I never could share the same kitchen even for a few hours."

"So why did you invite them?"

"I was trying to be nice. I knew they wouldn't come." Sylvia walked over and sat on Saul's lap. She blew in his ear. She tried to seduce him, but it didn't work. She knew he was worried about not being able to perform. "Darling, isn't it time you went to see a doctor? Maybe a doctor can help. You know it isn't good for a young married couple like us to completely give up sex forever."

"I guess you're right. I've been putting it off. Do you remember last time? Remember, I tried Viagra. Got some pills from a buddy of mine. At first, the Viagra seemed to work OK, but later I found I was allergic to it. That's when I had that fender bender. It was one of those drug reactions they

49

call 'side effects'. In fact, sometimes guys get color changes from Viagra. I didn't say anything about it at the time, but it happened to me. I was afraid to drive for almost a week because the red lights looked green and the green lights looked red. I'll talk to Harry. He and Rose moved down here before we did. Maybe he's found a good local doctor. I know one thing: we can't afford to get our car fixed every time we have sex."

8

At dawn on the morning of January twentieth, Inauguration Day, Rachel hopped out of bed and slipped on her robe as soon as the alarm went off at six A.M.

Standing at the window, she could see the gray spires of Georgetown University atop the high bank on the opposite shore of the Potomac River. From her vantage point on the Virginia side of the river she studied the university's mosque-like white domed observatory and its myriad of lesser buildings hanging like cliff dwellings above the river. It gave her the impression of a medieval citadel layered on a mountain wall. Rachel's eyes swept eastward past Key Bridge to the half-lit Washington skyline. She could see the gentle curves of the Watergate apartments on the opposite bank and the massive white box that was the Kennedy Center for the Performing Arts.

An unseen Potomac River was overlain by a low stream of fog flowing silently between the river banks and under the series of low bridges; then meandering around the curve near Reagan National Airport and becoming lost against a backdrop of haze in the distance.

Standing at the window, Rachel contemplated the serenity of the scene as her mind and spirit tried to capture the full significance of this day so especially meaningful for anyone related to David Fishman. As she stared at the awakening city, her mind picked over a store of daydreams among which were happy fantasies jumbled in with apprehensions. Rachel, a large woman, solidly framed, who towered several inches over her slight husband, Herman, exuded an aura of matronly middle-age. Her family and friends thought of her as intellectual, self-controlled, decisive and occasionally brusque, a personality to fit her build. To them, Rachel was the organizer, sure of what everyone else should do and where everyone else ought to be going. Underneath it all however, and particularly in recent years, Rachel was not very sure where she herself was going.

Now the years of her youth had slipped away, and as she found herself entering her twenty-third year of marriage to Herman, with a twenty-year old daughter, Marsha, it seemed to Rachel that the colors of her life had begun to run. Things she had always been sure of became tinted with memories now run together so as to be almost indistinguishable. The tough warp and woof of the fabric remained, but it was splotched all over with unfulfilled dreams, vague hopes, and not a few fears. And with so many intermingled hues, to what useful purpose could this cloth now be applied?

Of many reveries, Rachel held a special favorite. She envisioned herself on assignment for her country. She could see herself administering a

51

diplomatic post, but not in some godforsaken third world country awash in poverty and disease. Since it was a dream anyway, why not a major diplomatic post? Why not ambassador to an English-speaking country, or even a country in the Far East, perhaps Japan, Thailand or China? She was good with foreign languages; she could pick up the language and be conversant in a few months.

There was no doubt, to Rachel's way of thinking, that the four years spent majoring in political science at Hunter College, followed by selective additional course work, and extensive readings on her own over a number of years, coupled with plain old common sense, all added up to pretty substantial qualifications. Rachel asked herself that if diplomatic assignments required the skill to manipulate, cajole, and debate for the best possible deals for her country, who could do it better than she? Had she ever lost an argument?

Perhaps more realistically, she could also see herself accepting a less prestigious ambassadorial post in a small-ish, peaceful European country, possibly, Lichtenstein. Yes, a tiny but orderly country would be fine. She could be quite comfortable in the kind of country where they didn't go around burning American embassies. Even a consular post in a faraway but exotic place like Tahiti would be acceptable; that is, if America had a consulate in French Tahiti. She made a mental note to look that up. Yes, a tiny out of the way place would be fine. No one had ever accused her of being a snob, and despite her new blood tie to her cousin, the incoming president, she refused to become one.

But through her reverie, Rachel was aware of no practical way in which she could disclose her yearnings to serve her country in a diplomatic role. With the exception of a few years doing research in international law for that firm in New York she had no real foreign service experience. And that brief taste of international affairs was almost twenty years in the past. After that, her work had consisted mainly of running her home, raising her daughter and working parttime on the accounting and bookwork for her husband's construction business. The ridicule she might be forced to suffer by merely admitting her diplomatic ambitions would likely be more than she could bear.

Interspersed with daydreams, there occasionally flashed through Rachel's mind scenes of a more somber nature. Ever since she had learned of her cousin David's interest in the presidency, she had been concerned for his safety. Although her love for David was insulated by his remoteness, still she harbored fears that while the loss of him would be devastating to the country, it would be a double blow to her family. He, their one hope for rising above mediocrity, if suddenly struck down, gone, would leave many of them unable to reconcile why something unexpectedly good should have come to them only to be ruthlessly snatched away. If that happened, it would have been far better if David had simply remained buried in the pack of practicing New York lawyers.

Rachel thought she was probably more aware than anyone else in the family that potential assassins lurked around every corner. Sometimes in her dreams she was overpowered by the thought that it was going to be impossible for David, even given massive security protection, to escape hour after hour, day after day, running a risk in any public appearance, through four long years in the White House.

Rachel rarely mentioned her nightmares to anyone, especially her husband Herman, because she knew what his comment would be: "Why not let the Secret Service worry about that? They get paid for it. And they know what they're doing."

She might reply that they were supposed to know what they were doing when John Kennedy was assassinated, and Robert Kennedy, and when Ronald Reagan was shot, but how had that helped? Still Rachel knew that lacking the who, what, where and when of her fears, no one would listen to her. And even if they did, what could they possibly do? So she said nothing. But, being a great believer in ESP, her extrasensory perception told her something bad might be on the verge of happening.

Rachel walked over to the bed, reached under the blanket and grabbed Herman by the big toe. She twisted it, not hard enough to do damage, but firmly enough to give him the message that it was about time to get up. Herman yelled a loud: "Ai-yai-yai," sat bolt upright for a moment, then fell back and rolled over for a catnap as Rachel walked back to the window to continue her reverie.

Although she loved her cousin, David, and was proud of him, she was hurt that he virtually ignored the flesh and blood side of his family, her side. His moneyed in-laws seemed to monopolize his attention. With the exception of fairly frequent contact that he maintained with his mother and father, he had remained aloof from the rest of the family. Her first cousin, yet she hadn't seen him except on TV in over two years. When she and several relatives in New York gathered to place a congratulatory call to him right after the election, they said he was too busy to come to the phone and could he call back. But he never did call back. He had asked his mother Rose to call back for him. "But we talk to Rose all the time. And even after she and Harry moved down to Washington, we still talked to Rose once a week," Rachel said in a loud whisper.

"Who are you talking to, Rachel? Is there somebody else here?" Herman asked sleepily as he raised himself on one elbow.

53

"No," she answered softly, "it's just me."

"What are you doing?"

"Looking at Washington. What else?"

As Herman rolled over for another catnap, Rachel studied the brightening sky. It would soon be sunup. She thought about her brother, Hymie and his wife, Shirley. Good old Hymie. He had suggested that when the entourage came down from New York, they could all save a lot of money by staying at Sylvia and Saul's apartment in Silver Spring. At least ten people in a two bedroom apartment with only one bathroom! Rachel was emphatic. They were not going to take advantage of their younger sister. And they were definitely not going to wait in line to go to the bathroom. So Rachel took the lead as always and booked them all into the hotel, including Shirley, Hymie and their son, Arnold; her husband, Herman, her daughter, Marsha and herself as well as two dozen other relatives from out of town. Even Sylvia and Saul had decided to stay at the hotel because Saul said he would never be able to drive from Silver Spring to downtown Washington through Inaugural Day traffic without getting several tickets for illegal left turns. On top of that, they would probably have been redirected all over the place by the police and arrived hours late for the Inauguration.

But, Rachel thought, Hymie had not been satisfied. Was he ever? Since Sylvia and Saul's apartment would be empty, he insisted that he, Shirley and Arnold could stay there. It was at that point that Shirley put her foot down. In fact, she put her foot down right on his foot. She was not going to go grocery shopping, cook and clean up instead of staying at a hotel, eating out and having fun.

They came in from far and wide like a swarm of locusts. Shirley's brother, Ben, came in from Chicago, with his wife, Miriam, plus half-a-dozen of Miriam's relatives. Six of Miriam's brother's coworkers also came. From Miami came Celia and Jake and their four kids, kin of Herman's. Sometimes, Rachel thought, they must have emptied the west since so many relatives from the extended family were in from California, Arizona and Nevada. And after the hotel had booked fifty-four rooms just for the family, the management announced that they were full and had to cut off any new reservations.

Rachel heard a light tap on the door. She opened it to see her daughter, Marsha, standing on the threshold in her bathrobe with a cup of coffee. "Can I come in? I see Dad's still asleep."

"Yes, come in. Are you getting ready? What are you going to wear today? That new blue satin dress would be lovely."

"I'm not going."

So They Went and Elected a Jewish President

"Marsha, this is history in the making and this is a once-in-a-lifetime event for the family. Unless, of course, David gets re-elected. Then it would be a twice-in-a-lifetime event. You have to go. I insist." But Rachel had learned years before that changing Marsha's mind was like trying to break stone with a soggy bagel.

You couldn't tell by looking at her in her bathrobe with her hair undone and no makeup, but Marsha was a striking young woman, built like a very well endowed alabaster statue. She was not married, but she knew that back in New York she could have gotten married simply by picking up the phone and asking any one of a half-dozen assorted moon-struck young men to come right over and bring a ring. But Marsha was too sensible for that. She believed that marriage had something to do with love and she wasn't in love.

Although always impeccably coiffured when she went out, her hair was a mystery to her friends and dates. Amidst a profusion of wigs which she manipulated like a pea and shell game and frequent trips to Andre's where she went through a rainbow of colors, few knew the actual color of her hair.

Many thought Marsha to be beautiful, but while it is undoubtedly true that a Jewish girl with deep Caribbean-blue eyes, full dark lashes and a sensuous mouth, could drive men of all ethnic groups and even of non-ethnic groups crazy, Marsha was not a perfect beauty by some standards. Her beauty problem was minor, but it had something to do with the nose. A gourmet would have liked just a tiny bit less sour cream on his baked potato. Marsha told only her closest friends that when she got her hands on some money, she was going to get some of that sour cream removed.

Overall, Marsha Schlotzberg's face presented a tiny bit of a Barbra Streisand-ish look.

But, without the singing, of course.

"As I said, Mother, I'm not going! I intend to watch the whole thing on the TV in my room here at the hotel because mob scenes are not in my repertoire. I refuse to spend long hours traipsing around getting trampled, squashed, propositioned, groped, and very likely, cold, tired, hungry and thirsty, not to mention maybe having to use one of those disgusting portable outdoor johns. I need my creature comforts. I am content to watch history in the making on TV. Besides, grandma Momma and grandpa Poppa aren't going either. Why don't you get on their backs?"

"My mother and father both have health problems. Momma broke her hip and can't walk very far. Poppa has heart trouble. His legs hurt when he walks."

"Doesn't that tell you something about this family, Mother? If they flew down, why couldn't Rose and Harry take them in their limo? The White

House is schlepping Rose and Harry to the Inauguration in a limo, why can't they take grandpa Poppa— Harry's own brother?"

"Harry and my father are not on speaking terms. My father is upset that his son, my brother Hymie, can only find low-paying parttime jobs while Harry's son has a job for four years as president; eight years if he gets re-elected. Poppa says it isn't fair."

"But Uncle Hymie can't do anything. And neither can Uncle Saul by the way. Neither of them has been able to hold down a decent job in years."

"Hush your mouth! Times have been tough. The country has been in a recession. David will be trying to pull it out. And maybe he can do something to help Hymie and Saul find work in the government."

"Mother, you're a dreamer. David has said he is firmly against nepotism. I bet he won't give a job to a single person in this family."

Rachel's heart sank. She was hoping that if she ever got up the courage to talk to Rose about her aspirations, Rose might ask David to throw a little bit of nepotism in her direction.

*****

After a solid breakfast where one and all agreed they had eaten too much, Inaugural tickets in hand, the family gathered at the front entrance to the hotel.

Saul glanced around. "Imagine that," he said to Herman with a wink, "they didn't send a single White House car for us."

The doorman had bad news. He had called for taxis and a few had shown up, but none were willing to brave the traffic jams in Washington. And the family needed a fleet of cabs.

The men went into a football huddle in front of the hotel and came to a decision. They would drive. Saul had his own car, of course, while the others all had rentals. After counting heads, they saw they had enough cars.

As the nine car caravan crawled away from the hotel, Saul, in the lead car, drove slowly over Key Bridge to Washington. The following drivers, worried about getting lost in an unfamiliar city, kept close formation. A policeman on the bridge said they looked like dogs nosing one another's behinds.

As Saul drove around the circle of the Lincoln Memorial, he noticed police barricades set up on streets leading east from the circle in the direction of the Inauguration. He led the caravan around the circle three times while he tried to decide on another route. The caravan became so strung out, Saul, who was supposed to be in the lead, found himself following the last car around the circle, so, for a time, no one really knew who was in the lead.

Rachel, fidgeting in the back seat of Saul's car and concerned about the hour, asked if they could just park somewhere and walk to the Capitol Building.

"No way!" Saul replied. "Much too far."

Twenty minutes later, driving east along Constitution Avenue, they were detoured again and found themselves heading north.

"Are we getting closer?" Rachel asked.

"No, we're heading away," Saul replied in disgust. He could see Hymie waving his arms impatiently in the following car.

"Saul, you live in this city now. Don't you know how to get to the Capitol?"

"Sure I do. I know at least ten ways to get to the Capitol, but all of them seem to be blocked off."

Saul's cell phone rang. It was Hymie in the second car. "Saul, you've been driving like a spinning compass. I'm going to pull out front and take over."

But Hymie had to contend with his wife, Shirley. "Hymie, darling, you are not taking over! You're the guy who gets lost in his own hometown, and this place is loaded with No-Left-Turn signs, unreadable signs, double red lights. They want you to stop twice? And tell me, what do you do when you've got both a red and a green light staring at you? On top of that, cops on every corner telling you to go when the light is red and stop when the light is green. If I had my way, I'd be back at the hotel watching idiots like us on TV."

Hymie settled back down behind the wheel and chomped down on his cigar.

Finally, Saul managed to lead the caravan across town along K Street, where he turned south on North Capitol Street. No barricade. He sighed. "OK, folks, we're not far now. In the home stretch." He turned into a side street and wound up on a lot behind the city's main post office. The lot was plastered with No Parking signs. Penalties ranged from twenty-five dollars for usurping the spot of a minor post office official up to threats of 'No Mail Delivery For A Year,' the latter for taking slots assigned to higher officials.

"We can't park here," Rachel protested. "It is highly illegal. Look at those signs."

Saul looked over his shoulder at Rachel in the back seat. "It may be a bit illegal-ish, but it doesn't say anything about not parking on holidays like today. And if we don't park right now, we'll miss the Inauguration because we still have a twenty minute walk ahead of us."

The doors of the nine cars swung open simultaneously as the horde got out and began a forced march to the Capitol Plaza. They walked in the cold, cold weather. They walked into a wind that threatened to blow them back to the parking lot. Rachel tried to comfort those near her by saying that since they all held tickets, they would huddle together in their seats, hopefully not too far from the podium. She said there would surely be strategically placed outdoor heaters that would make it all quite comfortable. "Yes, Arnold dear, I'm sure they'll have vendors nearby where you can get hot chocolate. And I would love a cup of hot coffee."

But alas, it was not to be. Rachel was livid: "Tickets to stand? Whoever heard of tickets to stand? The tickets get you through the ropes, but they don't get you a seat? The recession is so bad the country can't afford folding chairs for the Inauguration?"

"What about the hot chocolate, Aunt Rachel?"

"The man says no vendors are allowed within a half-mile of the Capitol Building."

"Why?"

"Arnold, I don't know why. Maybe they don't think it's patriotic to have people chewing and getting mustard smeared all over their faces while the Oath of Office is being taken."

*****

Shortly before noon, the black presidential limousine drove down Pennsylvania Avenue to the Capitol. By this time, the Capitol Plaza was jammed as were the stands set up behind the white balustraded podium at which the ceremony would take place. The elevated stands on the steps of the Capitol Building were reserved to accommodate the members of Congress, the state governors, Supreme Court Justices, high ranking members of the military and international dignitaries.

The Marine Corps band played a brief fanfare as the new vice president's wife, then the new first lady, and after that, the new vice president came down the steps from the Capitol Building, each accompanied by a small group of escorts, to take their seats in the front row behind the podium.

At last, the outgoing president appeared and the new president, escorted by members of Congress and flanked by Secret Service men.

Standing just inside the ropes, Rachel and the family who had caravaned to the site were disappointed to find that they were so far away they couldn't see anything without field glasses. Happily, in the family alone, there were at least thirty field glasses, which were now all pointed in the direction of David Fishman who looked magnificent in the black silk top hat, white silk scarf and black topcoat.

Sylvia handed her glasses to Rachel. "And look at Rose and Harry sitting there, right in the thick of it, with important people on both sides."

"Why not?" Rachel said. "The least they can do is take care of the president's parents even though they make the rest of his family stand here a mile away."

"And doesn't Lisa look nice?" Sylvia commented.

Rachel zoomed the field glasses to close in on the soon-to-be first lady. "With all that money," she sniffed caustically, "even a hyena could be made to look nice. Her problem is her jaw isn't heavy enough to hold her snooty nose down."

After a series of invocations and band fanfares, the family stood spellbound as David Fishman was administered the Oath of Office by the Chief Justice of the Supreme Court. During the oathtaking, Lisa stood at David's side holding a Bible. People who were sitting close enough saw that this was not the traditional bible used by George Washington, it was the *Hebrew Bible.* When they saw it, the president's mother smiled; the president's father smiled; but the rest of the family was so far away they had no inkling there was an innovation in the oath-taking. All they could do was wonder whether a Jew was going to be sworn in on a Christian Bible.

Following the oath, there came a thunderous round of applause from the spectators, a flyover by a roaring squadron of military airplanes, and the distant boom of cannons from four miles away on the other side of the river: Fort Myer's traditional firing of the twenty-one gun salute.

As David began the Inaugural Address, the family stood listening at a nearby loudspeaker. But the loudspeaker sound was intermittent. No one could tell why. It was either due to an electrical short or from sound being blown away by the strong gusts of wind.

Arnold, standing next to his Aunt Rachel, was agitated. "You have the field glasses, Aunt Rachel, what is he saying? What is Cousin David saying?"

"Arnold, dear, I'm sorry but with this particular brand of field glasses you can *see* him better, but you can't *hear* him better. If I could read lips, I'd tell you."

So it was that about thirty family field glasses, trained on the podium, could see the Inaugural Address live, but family members could only hear snatches of it. Piecemeal phrases came through: "My fellow Ameri...," "My plan for the fu...," "Yes, America is on the threshold of...," "...golden opportu...,"

"...long history of...," "...from one ocean to...," "...unemploy...," "...taxes will be...," "...with labor and indus...," "...the Constitution and...," "Yes, for every one of you..." "Welfare should definitely be...," "... keep health high on..."

Saul looked at Hymie. "What did he say about taxes, Hymie? Did he say he was going to raise taxes or lower them?"

"Not sure, Saul. The crowd applauded, so I suppose he said he was going to lower them."

"And when he mentioned 'welfare,' did he say he was going to increase it or eliminate it?"

"Your guess is as good as mine."

Rachel was puzzled. "Saul, when he said 'health,' what did he say he was going to do about health care?"

"Rachel, I don't think he was talking about health care. I think he was talking about the country's health."

"You're both wrong," Hymie said in disagreement. "I think he was talking about the health of our exports."

Arnold piped up: "I heard him say something about sex."

"Arnold, darling," Rachel said, "I think he was only referring to the opposite sex."

"But I distinctly heard him say 'sex.' Wow!"

"Arnold, you haven't even had your Bar Mitzvah yet, so you don't know anything about sex...even if you do know all about it, you don't know anything about it, so just shut up."

Confusion reigned among the listeners. Rachel tried to comfort the group: "Later, we can ask Marsha what David said. She is watching the whole thing on TV at the hotel."

*****

The Inaugural Parade proved to be a test of who could stand long enough to watch it without getting frostbite. Halfway through, the snow began falling and the family, chilled to the bone, threw up their gloved hands and trudged back to the main post office parking lot. Some of the cars had threatening notes stuck under the windshield wipers, but happily none had police tickets.

The caravan managed to get out of the city and back to the hotel before the snow accumulated and traffic jams paralyzed the nation's capital.

*****

So They Went and Elected a Jewish President

As Rachel and Herman took the hotel elevator to the third floor where the ballroom was located, Rachel was unusually quiet.

"What's the matter, Rachel?" Herman asked.

"This whole Inaugural business is a disaster," she replied.

"What do you mean, a disaster?"

"From our standpoint, I mean. Here we are, relatives of the president no less, and we couldn't even get seats for his Inauguration. Then, the parade. "What a wonderful parade," everyone said. Again, no seats in the grandstand for the president's relatives. Holding a valid ticket, I am entitled to stand on a street corner."

"Maybe we should have stayed in New York," Herman offered.

"For once, Herman dear, you may be right."

"Well, the party will cheer you up. And who knows, David might come to the party after the fourteen Inaugural Balls he has to attend."

"That's another thing," Rachel said as they exited the elevator and stood outside the ballroom, "every one of us received invitations to attend one of the Inaugural Balls. Some of us even had our ball gowns picked out. I remember you had a rented tuxedo reserved. But what did we find out? We have to *buy* tickets. The invitation is an invitation *only to buy* tickets. And such tickets! A mere three-hundred-and-fifty dollars per couple."

Herman, trying to calm his wife down, tried to be philosophical: "Rachel, we'll have a nice time at the family party. We won't be jammed in with a bunch of strangers like at those fancy balls. They tell me the balls are so crowded that when you get in the door, you can't move. Two hours pushing and you haven't even gotten to the bar. Further, no one can even see what you're wearing because it's so crowded no one can see below the neck. It's like being on the Eighth Avenue Subway in Manhattan at rush hour, only instead of costing a token, it costs a small fortune."

*****

As they approached the ballroom, Rachel and Herman saw the big sign on the wall that announced the family party: *Fishman Family Presidential Inaugural Blast*. Inside there was bedlam as over a hundred of David Fishman's family and friends were busily talking, laughing, dancing and drinking.

Rachel and Herman saw their daughter Marsha on the dance floor. "Rachel, you're going to have to talk to her. Her dress is too small."

"What do you mean? It's the right size."

"With the low-cut top and the micro-mini skirt, there isn't enough material there for a large napkin."

"Herman, I've talked and talked and talked. I get nowhere. Marsha says it's the style with young women these days. You talk to her. Maybe she'll listen to you."

Herman shrugged his shoulders. He had been down that road before, the familiar one with the stone and the soggy bagel.

Marsha was dancing with a cousin from Arizona while two other young male guests were trying to cut in. One of the waiters and a bar tender were also hovering around, feverishly gesticulating in the hope that Marsha would notice them. As always, Marsha handled it very nicely. She told the young aspirants that the night was young and every one of them would get his turn.

*****

A number of women were talking in a knot on one side of the room while a number of men were gathered at the bar. Topics of discussion were covered with much nodding of heads and general agreement: the state of the economy...bad, unemployment...high, job opportunities...poor, productivity...low, interest rates...too high, taxes...terrible, foreign affairs...miserable, defense... weak, stock market...a crying damn shame, price of gasoline...a crime, the national debt...disgusting, the environment...filthy, the past administration...crooked, the Republican Congress...a do-nothing bunch.

Hope for the future under David Fishman's leadership: Wonderful! Wonderful! And even more wonderful...

*****

The pre-Bar Mitzvah boy, Arnold, was in a corner trying to describe sex to a younger boy who appeared to be about eight or nine years old.

"Arnold, are you telling me that my penis is not just used for peeing?"

"That's right. The same thing is used for sex."

"But why do people have sex? What's the point?"

"They do it to have babies and they do it for fun."

"Is it fun like on a roller coaster where you laugh and scream?"

"No."

"Then what kind of fun is it?"

"It's kind of hard to describe. I've never actually done it myself. An older guy told me about it. He said it kind of tickles."

"Tickles? I always laugh when I'm tickled. I don't understand how it can be much fun without laughing."

"Well, lemme see. This guy said it is the most fun you can have without laughing."

*****

Seeing Saul standing nearby, Rachel left the group of women and pulled Saul over into a corner. "Saul, do you believe in ESP?"

"Maybe yes. Maybe no."

"I am an ESP carrier. It's in my blood."

"So?"

"You live down here now with Sylvia. Herman and I are still in New York because of his construction business."

"So?"

"I am worried about David. My ESP tells me someone might try to assassinate him. Since you live here, I want you to do something about it."

"Rachel, what on earth can I do about it?"

"You can keep an eye on him. He does some risky things. For example, he still rides his bike in the streets. And the other day, he jumped out of a car he was riding in and ran into a Starbucks for carryout coffee. Maybe he has been able to pull this stuff off as president-elect, but now, as president, these things are too dangerous."

"Hey, Starbucks is hard to resist. But that kind of thing is dangerous, I agree. Tell me, what can I do about it?"

"Just keep an eye on him," Rachel ordered, as she turned on her heel and went back to the group of women.

Saul, who hadn't seen his cousin-in-law in years, wondered how that could be possible.

*****

Among the men at the bar the conversation soon turned to whether they should consider relocating to Washington to get in on what Hymie called 'the gravy train.' Hymie made it sound easy. A letter and resume to the White House was all that would be needed to land a high-paying government job.

One of the distant relatives named Sam, disagreed: "I'm from Arizona; I've been a Republican all my life and while I wouldn't mind working for a Democratic administration, when they saw my record, they'd tack my resume on the wall in a back room of the White House and take turns throwing darts at it."

A family member from Chicago named Max, also disagreed for another reason: "A letter and resume...baloney! When you saw how thick your completed application package had to be, it would take six-inch nails to hold it on the wall so they could shoot foot-long arrows through it. And frankly, Hymie, you can talk all you want, and maybe you do have an inside track, but let me tell you my story: right after the election, my business looked like it was going belly up. So, like you're suggesting, I did send a letter and resume to David's Transition Team leader, Roger Halstead. I got back in the mail a pack of forms three inches thick. They wanted to know about every school I went to starting in kindergarden, including my grades, my attendance record, the sports I played, and extracurricular activities. Next came work experience. I had to list every job I ever had, including my paper route as a boy, my duties, earnings, supervisors' names, and did I get promoted? If not, why not? Why I left for another job. Under business experience I had to list all my employees by name and state whether they had ever belonged to a subversive organization. I had to list my product lines and suppliers. Also, why the business folded or succeeded, if that was the case."

"But listen, Max," Hymie interrupted, "all that is stuff you should have at your fingertips. So, what's the big deal?"

"Wait a minute, I'm just halfway through. I had to give six character references, four work references, a bank reference, a statement from the local police and the state police. I had to list every psychotherapy session; that is, if I ever had psychotherapy and why I thought I needed it. And if I never had psychotherapy, why I thought I *didn't need it*. My marriage record, including any extra-marital affairs, even one-night stands, and full information on any children born out of wedlock. Thank God, I could leave all those lines blank except for details of my marriage which has been...well, that's another story."

"Are you finished?" Hymie asked impatiently.

"No. You're going to get the whole nine yards. They wanted a list of my hobbies, my health records, names of my doctors and dentists, names of every relative who ever held a government job, going back as far as my grandparents. Had I ever had a security clearance and if I didn't have one any more, why I don't still have it. Next, I had to list the names of every Russian, I ever met, every mainland Chinese, Libyan, Cuban, Iranian..."

"Stop," Hymie said. "Enough already. You've made your point. So there's some paperwork involved. I still think that having a relative in the White House will cut through all that red tape."

So They Went and Elected a Jewish President

"Well, if you find out how to do it, Hymie, be sure and let me know. I'll be waiting in my store in Chicago for you to call."

*****

As the evening wore on approaching eleven-thirty, there was rampant speculation about whether the president was going to make an appearance. Nobody cared much whether the first lady came with him, but they were all on pins and needles hoping President David Fishman would make an appearance, however brief.

At a few minutes before midnight, the small band played a fanfare, the doors to the party room flew open, the crowd rushed forward, and in swept Rose and Harry, dressed like royalty and exhausted, but still smiling. Someone shouted out: "Look everybody, the presidential parents!"

Someone else in the crowd said, "It's nice seeing the presidential parents, but I ask you, *where's the presidential?*"

Suddenly there was new life in the waning party as the shoulder-to-shoulder crowd gathered around Rose and Harry, many of the crowd calling out: "Is David coming?" and "When is David coming?"

Rose, in an impromptu speech, said that he sent his love; yes, he was aware that all of them were here in town celebrating in his honor. He sincerely thanked them and wished them all a wonderful time...

"But is he coming?" someone called out from the back of the room.

"No, he can't make it. He was exhausted and had to be taken directly back to the White House right after an appearance at the fourteenth Inaugural Ball." Rose went on to say that David had asked her to ask them to please listen to a special message he had prepared for the family. There was a hush in the crowd. Rose began reading the message in which her son wished each and every one of them a wonderful party and a pleasant stay in Washington, followed by an even more pleasant trip home. He hoped they could look forward to good and continuing jobs and businesses back home.

At that point, Sam from Arizona and Max from Chicago gave sidelong glances in Hymie's direction. Hymie pretended not to notice.

Rose continued: "David also wishes, and he says this is a strong wish filled with the highest aspirations, a wish that his new administration will have a successful four-year term in office in spite of serious problems in the nation and the world. He ardently wishes that all of his relatives and loyal supporters will get behind his imaginative new programs in the fields of health, welfare, tax reform, defense, the environment, and most importantly, education."

65

The message took a full ten minutes to read.

As the crowd broke up into little knots and the party wound down, Saul buttonholed Herman and asked him what he thought of David's message.

"Well, Saul, I thought it was very, very nice, but I wasn't sure whether it was intended for the family or for *both Houses of Congress.*"

So They Went and Elected a Jewish President

9

General Ali Karasek drove up Connecticut Avenue to The Forty Thieves where he sipped anisette and watched a succession of belly dancers lithely swivel their bejeweled omphalos across the stage to the accompaniment of the nostalgic sounds of bouzouki music. The night club was redolent of incense mixed with traces of what Karasek knew was hashish as he sat in a dark corner, well-removed from the crowd of patrons surrounding the stage. He lit a Turkish cigarette as he reflected on his past weeks in Washington.

Karasek remembered his chance meeting with the new president's relatives, the Steinbergs, in the coffee shop of the Continental Hotel on the morning of his arrival in the United States. He had gone to the coffee shop for breakfast and had stumbled on a gold mine. It was this meeting, in fact, that spawned an opportunity to gain the information he would need for an assassination plan.

Although he had not talked with the Steinbergs since that snowy day in November, he had carefully tracked their movements. He knew they had moved down from New York and now lived in a luxury high rise apartment in Silver Spring, a suburb of Washington, located just thirty minutes north of the White House. He knew which market they shopped in and the kind of car they drove. He knew their favorite kosher deli, Saul's preference for lox and bagel with a double helping of cream cheese and Sylvia's fondness for matzo-ball soup. He knew they usually paid the bill by credit card and left a modest fifteen percent tip in cash on the table. He had learned through sources that Sylvia Steinberg was not currently employed and also that she had worked long hours for her cousin's presidential campaign. Saul Steinberg was a recently terminated insurance salesman. He was currently attempting to organize an embryonic film production company.

As Karasek sipped his second glass of anisette, savoring its smooth, licorice-like flavor, his mind savored the knowledge that although the Steinbergs, close relatives of David Fishman, had not yet had any contact with the new president, sooner or later they must. Whereas less-experienced operatives paid scant attention to intimate details like those he had learned about the Steinbergs, Karasek knew that such information could be invaluable. The long range plan taking shape in his mind involved infiltration into the Steinberg family. Earlier, he had thought about acquiring similar information about the president's parents with an eye toward having an operative ingratiate himself with them. But he discarded this idea for two reasons: first, because the president's parents probably had some Secret Service protection. Thus, it would be dangerous to begin asking questions about them and tracking their movements; second, he had learned that Harry Fishman, after many years running stores in New York, was an alert observer of people and surroundings and had a somewhat suspicious nature. It would be almost impossible for anyone to get close enough to get any real information out of him.

Karasek's thoughts turned to the carton he had smuggled into Florida from the Middle East through Havana and which now rested in a secure vault in

67

Washington. The speedy plane, equipped with a high-tech covering of stealth radar absorbing material, had made the ninety-mile crossing from Havana, skimming the wave tops and slipping through the Americans' radar like a small fish gliding through holes in a fisherman's net. Karasek always smiled at the notion that if you greased enough palms, you could accomplish just about anything.

The contraband carton contained a substantial fortune in unmarked American bills, money that was intended to buy whatever might be needed for the assassination. But Karasek would see to it that most of this money would soon be resting in his personal account in a Swiss bank. This would be his secret, his alone. The other part of his plan involved two expatriate German engravers who, living in Nicaragua, had printed a like supply. They were, by all acounts, truly excellent imitations of American bills. These were also in a secure vault in Washington. The counterfeit money would fund the assassination.

A few years earlier it would not have been possible to distribute openly such 'money' right under the noses of U.S. Treasury agents, but times had changed. The U.S. Bureau of Engraving and Printing, suffering repeated budget cuts and besieged by employee demands for 'upward mobility,' was not printing the quality product it had formerly. As the old line of highly skilled, highly paid engravers were forced one by one into early retirement, they were replaced by upwardly mobile clerks and janitors who were trained virtually overnight in the profession. The new breed had taken over with work output hampered not only by lack of knowledge and uncertain skills but also by long coffee and smoke breaks, frequent bull sessions and time spent in lengthy phone calls to friends, families, lovers and bookmakers.

The resulting product was substandard to say the least. In fact, newly printed bills looked counterfeit to many people. When exchanged in banks in Europe and Asia, the new bills brought tears to the eyes of some of the world's leading engravers who remembered with nostalgia those former times when the U.S. Treasury had produced the Rembrandts and Renoirs in the field of money-making. And occasionally, the tears were those of laughter.

Karasek's two Nicaraguan-Germans had achieved the capability to make U.S. notes of far higher quality than the U.S. Treasury itself. But the cunning general knew he could ill afford to leave witnesses in place. Especially dangerous would be those who might be tempted to make a barrel of money for themselves, squandering it on mansions in Beverly Hills with swimming pools and lighted tennis courts and perhaps leaving a paper trail that could lead back to him.

Karasek traveled to Nicaragua for a long weekend ostensibly to take inventory and coordinate shipments. During his visit, he did only what he felt he had to do. Afterwards, the expatriate German engravers were quietly repatriated posthumously to their native land. Their bodies were accorded first class trips back to Munich where they were honored with tasteful and expensive funerals, all paid for with counterfeit euros that had been stored in shoeboxes in their print shop.

When the waiter at The Forty Thieves suggested another glass of anisette, Karasek hesitated a moment and then accepted. Why not, he said to himself. I've accomplished quite a lot in the past few months with very little time off. By the love of Allah with full deference to Abraham, Moses, and David, I deserve a night of relaxation.

As he was sipping his third glass, the general remembered an item he had to attend to. He had received word that Colonel Zumar Karam had arrived in town. The colonel was staying at the Zorita Hotel.

It was about eleven P.M. when the general stepped out of the club into the frosty night air burrowing his head down into his upturned coat collar as he dialed his cell phone. The hand holding the phone was in a warm glove but the other hand was so cold and the night so dark he angrily punched in the wrong number three times before he got the right one.

"Room 719 please," he said as he strolled down the street in the direction of the parking garage where he had left his car. The switchboard operator's voice carried a crisp pleasant tone that made it sound as if the caller had the Sheraton or the Hilton on the line, but Karasek knew the Zorita Hotel to be an ancient derelict in an impoverished neighborhood in southeast Washington. The hotel was owned and operated by a not-well-financed Iraqi immigrant.

Karasek recognized at once the voice on the other end of the line. There could be no doubt. It was Zumar. The hoarse intense whisper that came through the phone brought back memories of past assignments they had worked on together. He hadn't seen the tall slender Iraqi in several years, but Karasek could vividly picture the bald olive dome, the large bent nose, the black mustache that drooped down around a friendly smile and, most noticeably, the constant nervous fidgeting of a man who was as restless as a belly dancer facing an appendectomy, the scar from which could ruin a career. Strange for a man who was a colonel in the Iraqi army, assigned to intelligence duties. But, despite this, Karasek had a deep admiration for Zumar. He had high respect for the other's keen mind sharpened by long practice in espionage, and although Zumar customarily fretted and fidgeted through every job they had tackled together, things had always come out right in the end.

As Karasek suggested a meeting perhaps at the Zorita, Zumar curtly told him he had taken leave of his senses.

"But the hotel is owned by an old friend, a countryman of yours," Karasek argued genially. "Can't you trust him to set us up in a private room there?"

"On this job, I don't trust anyone."

"Come now, don't you even trust me, an old friend?"

"Not entirely."

Karasek smiled as he listened to the fretful voice coming through. Just like old times. "By the way, has our other friend arrived?"

"Yes, he's here."

"Well, about the meeting...tell you what, there is a restaurant downtown called the Purple Sphinx. Let us meet there tomorrow night."

"Is it a private club?"

"No, just a restaurant."

"You must be out of your mind," Zumar commented acidly. "Or drunk. Have you been drinking?"

"Just a couple," Karasek confessed. "But more than that I am filled with the heady aphrodisa of Middle East belly dancing."

The colonel was silent for a moment. Then, in a stern, gravelly whisper, he asked, "Well, if you're not drunk, why do you suggest a place like that? A restaurant? And on a Friday night? You can't be serious."

"On the contrary, I am serious. I am certain we can conduct our business there without being disturbed. You see, the Purple Sphinx has the worst food and service I have ever seen. Added to that, the prices are so outrageous no one goes there any more, so it is an ideal place to be alone."

The colonel finally relented.

"Well, goodbye then," Karasek said smiling into the phone. "I look forward to seeing both of you at the Purple Sphinx. Let us meet at 8:30. By the way, one other thing...a word of caution...make sure you both have something to eat *before* you come to the Purple Sphinx!"

* * * * *

The general walked to the parking garage near The Forty Thieves. He struck up a conversation with a young parking attendant, a Lebanese youth who was studying at a university in Washington by day and working nights to help pay his tuition.

As the youth held the car door open, Karasek settled into the driver's seat. Pulling the door closed, he slid the window down and studied the face of the young man who stood close at hand wondering how big a tip he had earned for providing the information.

"The Navel Jewel, you say?"

"Yes sir. It's only about ten minutes from here," the youth volunteered, trying to be as helpful as possible. "You go west on M Street, turn right on Wisconsin Avenue and it's only a few blocks from there."

Karasek peeled a twenty dollar bill from a roll, crumpled it, squeezed it into the young man's hand and drove off.

The Navel Jewel, on lower Wisconsin Avenue just above Georgetown, was a very small club specializing in Middle East fare and entertainment. On entering, Karasek took a table next to the slightly raised dance floor that doubled as a stage. He glanced around. With the exception of a small group of men huddled at a bar in the rear, he was the only patron. He studied the four musicians at the rear of the stage who were playing a pitiful imitation of bouzouki music. He decided he had made a mistake. A twenty dollar mistake at that, and rose to leave. Even though the money he carried was counterfeit, he still didn't like throwing it away.

A waiter appeared out of nowhere, blocking his way. "You can't leave without paying the cover charge."

"But I ordered nothing."

"No matter, it has to be paid as soon as you sit down."

Not wishing to make a scene, Karasek said quietly through gritted teeth, "Well, how much is it?"

"Twenty-five dollars."

Outraged, Karasek's fingers were closing around the dagger hidden in the folds of his jacket when a fanfare and the flash of colored lights introduced a raven-haired beauty who swept onto the stage. She let the pink veil slip provocatively from her face and smooth round shoulders as she began the slow, graceful movements that had driven more than one man to leave his wife.

Karasek slumped back down into the seat mesmerized.

"Her name is Helena," the waiter whispered.

Then, for almost a half-hour, Karasek sat entranced as the stunning belly dancer performed solely, it seemed, for him. At one point, she came up very close, and gazing into his eyes, provocatively slipped the veil over his head, then slowly let it slide away.

She is dancing for me alone, he thought. It never occurred to him that since his was the only shadowy outline the dancer could discern beyond the footlights, Helena had little choice.

Even the bouzouki music sounded better. Karasek was in Baghdad, he was in Riyadh...he was in the fabled lands of his youth. He smoked a Turkish cigarette, sipped his liqueur and nibbled on goat's milk cheese spread on tiny cut squares of pita bread as his eyes hungrily watched every movement of Helena's soft undulating body.

After the dance, she joined him for a drink.

"My dear, that was the most sensuous and poetic dance I have seen anywhere in the world," he told her with unbridled admiration.

"Thank you," the belly dancer replied with a smile and a look in her heavily mascara'd eyes that told him she was pleased by the extravagant compliment.

Later, in bed, belly-to-belly, she owned up that she was from Hartford, Connecticut, and her real name was Mary Shaughnessy. The admission came as no real surprise to Karasek, who might have liked to believe otherwise, and had almost convinced himself otherwise, but who still prided himself on his ability to spot a fake Arabian belly at a distance of two hundred paces, even in moonlight.

For his part, Karasek, who was smitten by the beauty and charm of the girl, owned up that he was not quite authentic himself, being only half-Arab, the other half being Jew. Under the spell of her beauty combined with the liqueur, he confessed to her that his entire life had been a succession of half-and-half likes and dislikes. He said he had developed real hang-ups over it. Smiling, he admitted, "I do half my work with my right hand, half with my left."

"What are you doing in this country? You don't mind my asking, do you?"

"Not at all. I am here to negotiate oil sales to America."

"Do you own oil wells?"

"No, I am only a representative."

"Well, I hope you'll sell us all you have. America really needs all the oil it can get."

"Unfortunately, I cannot sell America all I have. Considering the principles that have governed my life, I have decided to sell only half to the United States and half to other interests."

She was crestfallen. "You really are hung up on this half-and-half business, aren't you. Incidentally, I assume you know that I charge five hundred dollars for the night."

"Yes, but by the time we got here the night was half over. So, I hope you will be satisfied with two-hundred-and-fifty."

"That's OK as long as it's cash. I don't take credit cards."

"Cash, of course. And you are quite right about my hang-ups; for example, even in sex, it may sound crazy but half the time I like to be on top, half the time on the bottom."

"Well, that's no problem," she said laughingly as she clasped her arms around his neck.

And with that, they rolled over.

*****

At eight-thirty on the following night, General Karasek greeted Colonel Zumar Karam with a smile and a firm handshake at the entrance to the Purple Sphinx restaurant. The general was introduced to a man named Hassar, a beefy, muscle-bound Libyan who squirmed in an ill-fitting black suit. The dark flesh of the Libyan's fat neck bulged over his tight collar like a tire inner tube. He looked so much like a wrestler that Karasek's first reaction was to wonder whether the Libyans thought the best way to kill the American president was by squeezing him to death. Karasek dimly recalled having heard of Hassar but he was at a loss to recall in what connection.

As the trio entered the restaurant, Colonel Karam whispered to Karasek that the Libyan, as a matter of fact, had excellent credentials since it was he who did the job on the Israeli jumbo jet at Lod International Airport. Although Karasek nodded in apparent approval, the Jewish half of him would have much preferred hearing that Hassar had gained his credentials somewhere else like Paris, London, or Madrid.

Unmet by a maitre d' or waiter, none being in sight, the three men took seats at a table in the center of the large empty restaurant. Karasek and Colonel Karam talked over old times in guarded tones, with Hassar looking mutely on as the three sat toying with their silverware for almost twenty minutes. The men, surrounded by a sea of white cloth-covered tables, looked like explorers lost in the middle of a snow-covered plain. Karasek noticed that Colonel Karam was fidgety as always, dropping a fork on the floor several times.

Finally a waiter appeared, and almost at the same time, a thin elderly man in a gray tweed suit entered the restaurant. He took a table right next to theirs. Karasek scowled when he saw the man sit down just a few feet away. He whispered to the waiter that he and his companions would prefer another table, something over in a far corner.

So They Went and Elected a Jewish President

The shuffling of chairs was loud in the cavernous room as the men rose and followed the waiter to a table on the far side of the restaurant. As they were being seated, the general waved away the menus offered by the waiter. He looked up at the waiter coolly, "We've all eaten. Just bring us brandy and coffee; that is, if the coffee is fresh."

The waiter arched an eyebrow. "The coffee was made fresh this morning, Sir." He walked away piqued. To Karasek's surprise, the waiter appeared almost immediately and set the brandy and coffee on the table. As he did so, he intentionally jostled the table just enough so the coffee ran over into the saucers. Then he swung around and went to wait on the other customer.

Karasek made an effort to keep a pleasant look on his face, silently commending himself on his restraint. If a waiter had done that to him in the Middle East, he would have dragged him into the kitchen and scalded one of his feet in a pot of hot water while he simultaneously let the other one freeze in a bucket of ice. But this, he realized was not the Middle East. This was America where you had to put up with insults. He lit a Turkish cigarette. After a couple of puffs he felt more relaxed.

"Now where were we?" he asked. "Oh yes, about the plan. I have it all mapped out. I've been working on it pretty steadily since arriving here a few months ago. He'll be dead by May."

"May?" Colonel Karam asked incredulously. "But this is February! Why so long? We can surely do it faster than that. Remember, the bird of prey is swift on the wing. The slow arrow falls harmlessly into the sand short of its target. The lazy camel gets no...."

"May!" Karasek said sternly, his pleasant look disappearing. But the colonel was unmoved. "It is risky being in this country. Let us get it over quickly and get out."

Hassar grunted agreement as he sipped his coffee from the saucer, his tiny black eyes darting quickly back and forth from one man to the other.

The cunning and methodical General Ali Karasek had cut his teeth on treachery; he loved espionage; he loved sabotage; nothing pleased him more than a dangerous assignment in intelligence or counter-intelligence. But there was one thing he could not tolerate: arguing. He angrily jammed his cigarette into the saucer of his coffee cup. "How much simpler it would be, Zumar," he said, "if I had taken this job by myself."

The colonel stood his ground. He angrily pushed his chair away from the table, folded his arms and crossed his legs. Hassar tried to mimic the move but his thighs were so thick his top leg kept sliding off. However, Karasek got the message. He was outvoted. "So what do you propose?"

"A quick strike," Colonel Karam replied flatly.

"How clever," Karasek said sarcastically. "But let me ask a few simple questions: "Zumar, my friend and longtime associate, kindly tell me how, where and when?"

Before the colonel could answer, Hassar stood up heavily from his chair and started for the men's room. As soon as he was out of earshot, Karasek leaned over close to Colonel Karam. "Tell me, what does that big oaf bring to

73

the operation?"

"Don't underestimate him. For one thing, he's an explosives expert. For another, he's a pilot."

"Flying exactly what kind of airplane?" Karasek asked unconvinced.

"Small planes, big planes, even helicopters."

Pulling his chair back to the table and leaning over close to Karasek, Zumar whispered, "Ali, my old friend, look at it this way. We've got to be swift about this job. What if someone else kills him first? If that happens, we don't get paid."

"Who else would try to kill him? He is on friendly terms with the Russians, the Chinese, all of Europe, Southeast Asia...almost every country you can name. And we represent the few countries who want him out of the way."

"No, I don't mean other countries," Zumar argued. "Look, he's a Jew. There must be millions of Catholics and Protestants in this country who would like to see him wrapped in a sheet in a pine box."

Karasek's tone was mocking. "That's ridiculous. It shows how little you understand of the politics in this country. He was elected by the Catholics and Protestants. The Jews, after all, are only a tiny minority; possibly five to eight million at most in a country approaching 300 million."

"Well, what about the blacks?"

"He is the darling of the blacks. Let me give you an example: they used to have a president named Clinton who, although white, was a favorite of the blacks. And Fishman is perhaps even more of a favorite. To a black, he is what they refer to as a 'soul brother.' No Zumar, I must disagree. In this country only a zealot or a madman would be after him, and with all the security, such a one would find it virtually impossible. Please do not tell me we have to hurry because of the competition. There is none."

When Hassar returned from the men's room, Karasek attempted to attract the waiter's attention to order another round of brandy. The men watched in dismay as the waiter picked up the plate and coffee cup of the diner who had been sitting next to them before they changed tables, and moved him to a table just a few feet from theirs.

Drumming his fingers impatiently on the table, Karasek called the waiter over. He whispered sternly in the waiter's ear. "Why did you move that man right next to us? Could he be trying to pry into our private conversation? That's very impolite, you realize."

The waiter stepped back to the other table, whispered briefly to the elderly gentleman and then returned. He whispered in Karasek's ear: "The gentleman says he is lonely, Sir. And if you will bear with him, he will be finished in a few minutes. All he ordered was coffee and a piece of carefully aged, four-day-old pumpkin pie, a favorite of his and I might add, a specialty of the house. Then he will leave and then you can talk without anyone hearing you because I'll just go back to the kitchen and continue my poker game with the cook."

As the waiter turned to go back to the kitchen, he glanced over his shoulder at the three men, and in a supercilious tone added: "Come get me if you need me."

The three sat quietly but not patiently until the man at the next table finished eating. Leaving the money to cover his check on the table, the man stood up. He curled his mouth into a smile, bowed slightly in the direction of his three neighbors, a murmur of thanks on his lips, and letting out a belch that reverberated like a gunshot in the far corners of the large empty restaurant, strode out.

The conspirators finally agreed on a compromise. They would continue developing a methodical plan for an assassination in May, but would also make a quick strike in about a month.

As the meeting broke up, Karasek found himself moderately satisfied with the compromise. He recognized an element of added risk if the first attempt should fail, but on the other hand, he knew that a later attempt, if well planned, increased the ultimate probability of success. As a member of the intelligence community, he was familiar with the tried and true, world-renowned American proverb: 'If at first you don't succeed, try, try again.'

As the trio prepared to leave the restaurant, the burly Hassar grunted and then went back to the kitchen. Grabbing the waiter by the scruff of the neck, he dragged him out to their table. The waiter presented them with a check for almost a hundred dollars, which included a twenty-five percent tip.

"That's outrageous," Colonel Karam complained angrily. That much for poor service, a few glasses of brandy, and some stale coffee?"

But Karasek, now in a somewhat jovial mood, said, "Give me the check. Since I selected this place, I will pay the bill." He peeled a counterfeit hundred dollar bill from a roll in his pocket and threw it on the table. "After all," he said, "it could have been worse."

"How could such an outrage have been worse?" the colonel asked hotly.

"Very simply, my friend. It could have been a hundred dollars worth of food followed by several days of diarrhea."

10

Saul glanced up at the sign as he opened the door: *PLAIN AND FANCY COFFEE SHOPPE AND RESTAURANT*. And just below it, a small sign read: Anyway you like it...PLAIN or FANCY. The restaurant struck him as a comfortable, homey little place, clean and pleasantly decorated. He slipped into a quiet corner booth.

Saul was happy to see that the restaurant was almost empty and that the backs of the booths were quite high. He felt free to look over the Organ Transplant Society literature without concern over someone getting an accidental look. The doctor had sent him the material in an unmarked brown wrapper, the way magazines are carried out of an adult bookstore. Saul wasn't sure what was inside the wrapper but he didn't want to take any chances.

A squat, blonde waitress with a bouffant hairdo from which stray wisps of hair hung down having eluded her hair spray, walked over to the booth. Although she was chewing a massive wad of gum, she had learned a long time ago how to speak through it. "What would-juh like, honey? Ready for a big fancy dinner?"

"Gosh no. I'd just like a cup of coffee."

"How did-juh want it, plain or fancy?"

"What's the difference?"

"Plain is with milk...in...you know, a regular cup, and fancy is in a pretty mug with whipped cream on top."

"Oh, what the hey, I guess I'll take it fancy."

"Would-juh like a nice piece of pie with that? We have delicious home-made pie."

"Well, yes. That sounds good. Let me have some apple pie."

"Plain or fancy?"

"What's the difference this time?"

"Plain is just the plain pie, but fancy is a larger slice with a scoop of vanilla ice cream on top and topped off with a cherry."

"Well, better make that plain."

The waitress turned to leave.

"Oh, and Miss, may I have a glass of water?"

She looked back. "How did-juh want it...plain or...? Oh, all right."

As he sipped the coffee, Saul slipped the brochure out of the wrapper. The cover was slick white and embossed with raised gold letters...

THE GIFT OF SEXUAL LIFE

ANNOUNCING
AN
IMPORTANT NEW ORGAN BANK
For Recipients as well as Donors

For people from all walks of life
And all ages ***
If you are a recipient we *Guarantee* Happy Days Ahead!
But for others...
Did you know there is an art to giving?
It is so easy to receive but it takes much more to give!

YOUR GIFT WILL BE TRULY CHERISHED
BY
ONE LESS FORTUNATE THAN YOU

***Under twenty-one must be accompanied to doctor's
office by parent or guardian

Skimming through the brochure, Saul saw that it was filled with color photographs that would be judged obscene by any court in the land, but what bothered him most was the somewhat over-enthusiastic advertising. The brochure brassily advertised the happy, glowing reactions of recipients but was noticeably lacking in testimonials from donors. He wondered about that. A convict could make a donation and get out of jail, but if he committed another crime, he had nothing left to give for another release. And the men who took cash in return for their donation, would find that when the money was spent, not only would their pockets be empty, so would their pants.

Saul read a testimonial from a Mr. J.D. in Salt Lake City: "I'm seventy-four years old, but I keep six women happy in my building at the Golden Age Rest Home. I can't thank the Organ Transplant Society enough for giving me a new lease on life."

Another one read: "After getting my new organ, did I ever make sweet music!"

"Good grief," muttered Saul, "here's one from a woman."

Mrs. R.Q. Sioux Falls..."When I first heard about this thing, I figured, like most things, women would just be left out. But, believe it or not, there is an organ transplant for women! Most state laws do not permit my describing the details here, but let me tell you it's great. It works just fine! Gals, stop playing second fiddle to some young chick, see your OTSA doctor and give your husband's girlfriend a run for his money. If, on the other hand, you're sick of being a woman, an OTSA doctor can take care of that too."

As he paged through the brochure, Saul was startled by a sharp tap on the shoulder. It was Harry. He took a seat opposite Saul in the booth. "Saul, I'm sorry I'm late but Rose and I have been very, very busy lately. Too busy, in fact. What did you want to see me about? And what are you reading, *Playboy*? If those are pictures of what I think they are, it looks more like *Playgirl Magazine* to me."

"No, Harry, it's a brochure from that doctor we met at the embassy party."

Harry had a puzzled look on his face. "Saul, explain to me again about that doctor's name."

"You mean Doctor Doctor?"

"Yes. I have heard that when people get two doctors degrees, some of them like to be called Doctor Doctor. I guess they're trying to get full credit for their accomplishment. Does that doctor have two degrees?"

"No. He's just an M.D. His name is Doctor John Doctor. You see, Doctor is his family name."

"So, you might say, he was a doctor *before* he was a doctor?"

"Yes, I guess you could say that."

Saul saw the waitress walking over to their booth. "Watch out, Harry, here comes Miss Plain or Fancy."

"What did you say?" asked Harry.

"You'll see."

"Well hello," she said through a pink wad of gum that looked more massive than before. Although Saul snapped the brochure shut, the waitress got a quick look. She gave Saul a sly wink. "Don't leave that magazine behind when you leave, I don't want to get arrested."

"It's a brochure, not a magazine."

"Oh sure, and my name's Queen Elizabeth." Then, looking at Harry, the waitress asked, "What would-juh like, Hon? Ready for a big fancy dinner?"

"No thanks," Harry said.

"Oh, then you just want it plain?"

"No, I don't want dinner at all."

She stared at him, the gum bulging from her mouth like a partly deflated rubber ball. "Well, can I bring you anything fancy?"

"No, I just want something very, very plain: Nothing."

"You don't want anything? God, how does a person make a living around here?" As the waitress walked back to her station behind the counter, she muttered, "They come to a restaurant, not to eat, just to talk and look at dirty pictures."

"Harry, I asked to meet you because I have a problem. It's tough to talk about. I don't even know how to begin."

"Well, as the saying goes, begin at the beginning."

"At the beginning, everything was fine; it's lately that I'm worried about."

"Tell me this: Is it above the waist or below?"

"It's below."

"OK, now we're getting somewhere."

So They Went and Elected a Jewish President

"Now tell me: Which room of the house is it in?"

"The bedroom."

"Sylvia's pregnant."

"No, that's not it, and if she were, I'd be happy."

"So tell me, you and Sylvia want a child but can't conceive."

"No, we're not hung-up on having a child."

Harry leaned forward looking Saul in the eye. "I'm all out of leading questions, so if you don't tell me, I'm leaving."

Saul took a sip of his coffee, nibbled on the pie the waitress had brought, squirmed, and then blurted it out: "I'm having trouble performing in bed."

"I know you love Sylvia, so it couldn't be that. Tell me this, Saul, how old are you?"

"I'm thirty-eight."

"And you're having trouble in that department? Let me give you a little tip. Take a warm bath just before. It'll relax you. And put wheat germ on everything you eat. You can sprinkle it on your cereal in the morning, you can put it on toast, ice cream, steak, many things."

"Thanks for the tip, but I think my problem is a little bigger than just sprinkling a little wheat germ around."

"Saul, I know this is a tough time for you. You moved down here just a short time ago; you're probably exhausted. And I know you and Sylvia are worried about money. These things can have a psychological effect."

"How do you know so much about this stuff?"

"Remember, although I only ran a candy-store, I got to read all the magazines free. Every month: *Fitness and Health, Eating For Health, Not Eating For Health, Sex and Health*...you name it. Well, maybe you should see a doctor. At least get a physical and rule out that kind of problem."

"That's what I wanted to talk to you about. Since we just moved down, I haven't found a doctor here yet and I don't want to take a chance looking in the Yellow Pages. So, I was wondering what you thought about me going to see that doctor we met at the embassy party. You know, Dr. Doctor."

"So, you think that screwy doctor can help? Is that where you got the dirty magazine?"

"I called his office and they sent me a brochure. All I want him to do is check me over and give me some advice. Maybe a referral or something."

"Well, he is some kind of specialist in what goes on below the waist. He might have some ideas. By the way, he keeps calling me trying to get through to David, but I'm not in a position to help him get access. And I wouldn't if I could. And also, by the way, David came to our apartment for shabbat dinner last Friday night. Did I tell you? Our neighbors are mad as hell. No one could get into or out of the building while he was there. Secret Service agents on every floor. Cars on the street were being towed away just in case one of them might have a bomb. The building manager said that while he was flattered that the president paid a visit, there were so many complaints, he said he would appreciate it if Rose and I would maybe meet David at a restaurant or maybe we could eat at the White House."

"What about Lisa? Did she come?"

"No way! She's too snooty to be seen with Rose and me."

"But don't you see her at the White House?"

"We haven't been to the White House. At least, not yet. But David will be living there for four years. It could happen eventually. Oh, of course we go to a lot of embassy parties because those ambassadors are a lot like Doctor Doctor. They think they can get access to David through us. What a laugh. But Saul, we're off the subject. We were discussing your problem. So, again I say, go see him, what have you got to lose? Now, I really have to leave."

Saul picked up the check, folded the brown envelope containing the brochure and stuffed it into his overcoat pocket. Then he and Harry walked over to the cashier. As they approached, they heard the blonde waitress talking to the cashier: "I've been dating two guys lately. One of them has a very plain apartment, but the other one...Wow...are his digs ever fancy!"

Saul handed the cashier a five dollar bill saying, "I had a cup of coffee, fancy, and a piece of pie, plain."

The cashier looked at Harry. "Where's your check?"

"I had something very, very plain," Harry said. "I had nothing."

11

In the small outcroppings of the South Mountain range called the Catoctin Mountains near the Pennsylvania-Maryland border, there sits a secluded retreat known in Franklin Roosevelt's days as Shangri-La and later renamed Camp David by Dwight Eisenhower. Later presidents had not seen fit to tamper with the name of the camp, nor did David Fishman who counted it a pleasant coincidence that the camp bore his own name.

This place, where presidents go to relax from the pressures of office and where rambling informal meetings take place with foreign heads of state, lies about a half-hour helicopter flight from the White House.

It is not an uncommon sight to see two of the presidential eggshell-white-over-slate-gray helicopters chopping their way through the air about a mile or so off to one side of Interstate 270. The route runs north from Washington to Frederick, Maryland, where it changes to Route 15 that runs up past the town of Thurmont and close to the mountain hide-away.

On a chilly Saturday morning, forty-five days after David Fishman took office, two men trudged through deep underbrush. The going was slow because the equipment they carried was heavy and somewhat bulky. A helicopter stood in a small clearing a short distance behind the men, its rotor turning slowly. The pilot was a beefy-looking brute who sat half-asleep at the controls waiting for the men to return.

As the men struggled with their loads, their boots snapped through brittle winter underbrush strewn on the frozen ground.

Occasionally, the men would stop to rest, gingerly lowering their canvas-covered loads to the ground. Despite the thirty- degree cold, General Karasek had to wipe a trickle of perspiration that collected under the collar of his bulky parka. The rough gray-brown clothing camouflaged Karasek and Colonel Zumar Karam in the thicket, making it unlikely they could be seen from a hundred feet away except when they moved. Finally, they reached a small clearing, one that had been staked out in advance. Zipping open the canvas bags, each man removed a version of a Stinger missile, and began snapping some pieces into place. The heat-seeking missile was designed to home in on the exhaust gases of the target. The presidential helicopters were known to fly at a fairly low altitude, well within the altitude capability of their missiles.

Two presidential helicopters always flew in tandem. It was part of the security plan since no one would know which helicopter contained the president. Karasek and Colonel Karam overcame this obstacle by planning to fire a missile at each helicopter.

As the presidential helicopters came into view, at first no more than faint specks on the tree-lined horizon, the men made final preparations for launching their weapons. In a few minutes, a chopping sound came pulsing through the cold, still air. The helicopters, like game birds in flight over the woods, approached low in the sky about a quarter-mile east of the clearing. The men suddenly stood erect, each with a weapon mounted on his shoulder. Their feet were in a wide, braced stance. Each took careful aim through his telescopic sight and squeezed the trigger. Almost simultaneously, a ball of flame spouted rearward as each rocket lurched free of its restraining tube and whooshed into the air.

Without waiting to see the result, the men rushed back through the woods carrying the now-empty weapons. As they reached their helicopter, they threw the weapons and empty sacks into the back and clambered aboard. Hassar grunted and powered up the rotor to max takeoff revolutions. The helicopter was soon airborne and heading west, skimming the treetops to a hidden location in the hills of West Virginia.

*****

Karasek stood next to the potbellied stove warming his hands as Colonel Karam fiddled with the radio. Hassar handed each of them a cup of coffee laced with brandy. Glasses raised, they saluted the success of the mission. Now they could leave this cold, damp Allah-forsaken country and return to the cozy warmth of the Middle East where they anticipated receiving handsome rewards.

Karasek was beaming. "Zumar, my old friend, you were right. You were absolutely right. A quick strike. Carefully planned, of course, but not dragged out for months on end. My congratulations to you and Hassar...and to myself, of course."

The music on the radio suddenly cut off. "We interrupt this broadcast to announce Breaking News. An assassination attempt was made on the president just a short time ago. Happily it failed. Details are sketchy but sources tell us that missiles were fired at the president's helicopters as they were flying from the White House to Camp David. Several hundred police and Secret Service investigators are now combing the woods where the assassins were thought to have launched their weapons. It was clearly a multiple launch according to authorities. Sources also tell us that because the assassins were unsure about which one of the two helicopters carried the president, they had apparently attempted to shoot down both..."

"We did shoot down both," Karasek said grinning. "Of course, after firing the weapons, we had to run quickly back to our helicopter and although we did not actually see the missiles strike the president's helicopters, we heard them explode. Shut the radio off, Zumar. So they say it failed. Obviously a cover-up until they can decide what to tell the public."

"Wait a minute, Ali. Here's another announcement."

"President Fishman, interrupting a meeting at Camp David, when told the details of the assassination attempt, merely shrugged it off. He was quoted as saying it was all part of the job. But he was happy that the pilots and crew and visiting dignitaries all escaped injury when the missiles failed to hit their targets."

"What do you think, Ali? Is he alive or dead? This last report does not sound like a cover-up. In any case, how long could they carry on a cover-up? The supermarket tabloids would dig out the news in twenty-four hours."

The general's face grew somber. "You may be right, Zumar. Our preparation and launching were without flaw. We made no mistakes.

So, I can only conclude that if the missiles failed to hit their targets it was simply because there was something wrong with the missiles. Perhaps our fat Libyan friend here can tell us more about the missiles. You guaranteed to us that the missiles were one-hundred percent accurate. What about that Hassar?"

"I still guarantee that the homing devices in the missiles were perfectly accurate."

"How can this be? Explain yourself."

"If the missiles attained the correct altitude, they would have certainly hit their targets. In this regard, they are foolproof."

"So, how is it then that the targets were not be destroyed?"

Hassar got up from his seat and began pacing the floor. He grunted several times. Finally, he said, "It may be that the rocket motors did not have enough thrust."

Hungry for news, Zumar turned on the radio again. "Now for an update on the assassination attempt on the president. The Secret Service, working with the Maryland State Police have discovered two burned areas on a farm east of Route 270 where the assassins' missiles apparently exploded harmlessly on impact with the ground. Happily, there were no injuries. Fragments of the weapons are being collected and will be taken to the FBI lab to examine them for evidence of where they were manufactured. We now return to our regular broadcasting..."

Although Karasek was still unsure of the success or failure of their attempt, he began to believe that it had probably failed.

Colonel Karam, convinced that the attempt had failed, was seething. He left the other two and walked out onto the porch of the cabin. He had argued about not using high-tech weapons like the Libyan missiles. Too many things could go wrong. He much preferred simple weapons, like a pistol or rifle, even a dagger if one could get in close enough. Of course, with such weapons, the chances of getting away were not good...unless perhaps there was a carefully planned diversion. The one he liked best was to get close to the targeted victim as he left a hotel or office building. Just before the strike, a well-endowed young woman would be stationed in the vicinity who would casually slip off her jacket complaining about the warm weather and revealing her buxom, bra-less femininity under a gossamer sheer blouse. The diversion would only be credible, of course, in warm weather. But it was an effective diversion because not a single man guarding the president would be paying any attention to the assassin. Further, after the deed was completed, not a single man would be able to positively identify the woman's face.

* * * * *

As the three assassins lounged around the potbellied stove finishing their second coffee and brandy, a later newscast divulged that the missiles had missed their targets because defensive devices, which decoy missiles, had been employed on the presidential helicopters.

"So," Hassar said triumphantly, "the fault was not with my Libyan missiles."

"Oh yes it was," Karasek countered. "If your missiles were not so dumb they would have found a way around the defenses."

12

Saul entered the doctor's office. Not knowing what to expect, he was pleasantly surprised to find that it was very modern and handsomely furnished. At the embassy party when he first met the doctor it crossed his mind that the doctor might be operating on a shoestring, and Saul would not have been too surprised to find Dr. Doctor practicing in a basement broom closet.

A very good-looking receptionist took Saul's name and asked him to take a seat. Not knowing how long he'd have to wait, Saul looked around for a magazine. Nothing lying around except copies of the OTSA brochure which he had already read. He thought about picking up one of the copies lying on the table next to him and glancing through it again, but he was too embarrassed to do it because the receptionist seemed to be watching him. The only other patient waiting was an elderly man who looked up from the brochure he was reading, smiled wanly at Saul and returned to his reading.

As Saul glanced around the waiting room he had to admit the doctor seemed to have a plush operation going. A large bronze plaque mounted on the wall proclaimed that Doctor John Doctor was Board Certified in Sexual Organ Transplants by the Sex Organ Bank Division of the Organ Transplantation Society of America. Another smaller plaque simply read: John Doctor, Chairman, S.O.B. Division of the O.T.S.A.

A few minutes after Saul was seated, a nurse came from an inner office, whispered to the receptionist and then said: "Mr. Johnson, you're next. Follow me, please." She stepped forward to assist the elderly gentleman as he struggled to get up from his chair and steadied him as they walked slowly to the door leading to the rear of the suite.

Poor old geezer, Saul thought. One thing for sure, he didn't come to donate. You can practically hear his bones creak when he walks. Looks like he's ninety. Saul also noted that the nurse was really the one worth watching. She moved like a lynx, the thin white uniform covering her contours like a film of paint.

Saul saw that the receptionist managed to keep busy typing letters and talking on the phone, all the while working on her nails, hair and makeup. When she hung up the phone, he walked over to the counter. "Miss, do you mind my asking if you know anything about this society and what you think of it?"

"Not at all," she answered. "The doc's a real sweet guy, but I'm getting out of this dump."

"Why?"

"Simple. It doesn't pay anything. You see all these letters I'm pumping out here? Almost every one of them asks for money. You know, if you listened to the doc talk, you'd think the country was going wild over this thing, kind of like the way people went wild over Viagra. But I'm afraid that's not the case with this transplant stuff. He's having trouble just getting money to get the thing organized."

"Sorry to hear that. Got another job lined up?"

"You bet. I'm getting married."

"But that doesn't pay anything at all."

"Money isn't everything. I'm marrying one of the doc's former patients. In fact, this sweet guy was his very first, and it's only taken a few weeks for the black and blue marks to disappear. Sandra, she's the nurse who was out here a minute ago, and I, competed like hell for him, but I won. She's made it miserable for me here ever since, so I'll be happy to get out. Yeah, the doc's a swell guy; we owe it all to him. He made the guy I'm marrying into Hercules and Superman all rolled into one. Now, I don't know why you're here, aah... Saul, but if you're here as a recipient for an organ, you'd better watch out for Sandra, 'cause she said pretty emphatically that the next one off the assembly line is hers."

"But you mean the doc has only done one so far? He made it sound like a going thing."

"Yeah, he's like that. A real salesman. But of course, it is a nationwide organization and I understand a group of doctors on the west coast have done a couple. So, there's a few around all right. But Sandra said she doesn't want to travel all the way to the west coast to find a guy. She'd rather wait it out here."

"I see," Saul said as he thought about how nice it was that they all seemed to be on a first name basis, including him.

The nurse, Sandra, appeared. It was Saul's turn. Sandra and the receptionist exchanged sneers as Saul was ushered into an examination room, which was furnished in the usual way: examination table, medicine cabinet, sink, a chair for the patient and a small stool.

"Please sit down, Saul," Sandra said as she sat on the small stool and propped a clipboard on her knee. Now Saul, your last name is Steinberg, right?"

"Yes, that's correct."

"Now let me explain a feature of this office. Most other doctors' offices make you sit outside and on a first time visit, fill out a bunch of papers that would make a phone book look thin."

"Yes, I know. I've been down that road before."

"You'll be happy to know that Dr. Doctor doesn't operate that way. He wants the first contact to be personal. He feels he can learn a lot more about a patient if we do it this way."

"Fine."

"Now, Saul...your age is?"

"I'm thirty-eight."

"Good. We're off to a good start." said Sandra with a broad smile as she made a notation on the form on the clipboard.

"Single, married, or divorced?"

"Married."

Sandra's smile disappeared as she shifted uncomfortably on the stool and checked off the box marked 'married.'

"Saul, are you here as a donor or recipient?"

"Well neither, actually. I only came for advice from the doctor and perhaps a referral."

"You could have gotten a 'referral' as you call it from the Yellow Pages."

"Yes, but you see I met the doctor at a party and I merely thought I could talk to him about my aah...problem and get his advice."

"So you admit that you do have a problem..." Sandra mouthed the words about there being a 'problem' as she made a notation on the form. "Thirty-eight and pooping out a bit early, aren't you?" she whispered through a slight grin.

Saul reddened.

"Sorry, the doctor warned me to write these things down with my mouth shut."

"I should think you would," Saul said, growing somewhat irritated.

"How long have you been pooping...sorry, I should say, How long have you been experiencing difficulty?"

"Just the past month or two. You see, my wife and I recently moved down here from New York and I've started a new business, and all in all I may just be overtired."

"What business are you in?"

"Movies. I just started producing movies, you know, as an independent."

Sandra's face turned imperceptibly to the side as she shifted on the stool. She had always been told the camera favored her left side. She crossed her legs to show a bit more thigh, although she was well aware that if this guy was pooping out, he might not even notice.

"Now, Mr. Producer...I mean, Mr. Steinberg, I need to get some measurements."

"Good grief. Why do you need measurements? I'm only here for advice."

"Look my job is to completely fill out this form."

Saul didn't say anything, but it occurred to him she filled out her form nicely. In fact, somewhere down the line he might be able to use her in one of his movies.

"So, rest easy, all I need are a few basic body measurements. Your height and weight?"

"Six-one and a hundred-eighty pounds."

"Chest size?"

"Forty."

"Is that inhale or exhale?"

"Dunno. It's the size of my T-shirts."

"I see. Forty, exhale."

"Waist?"

"Thirty-seven."

"Is that before or after dinner?"

"It's the size of my shorts."

"Before dinner," she mouthed as she wrote the data on the form.

"Distance from navel to lower tip of back verterbrae?"

"Which way?" he asked. "Around the side or...?"

"It's down the front, back under the 'you know what,' and up the rear."

"That's what I was afraid of. Let's see...it's probably...hmmmm." He looked down at himself trying to gauge what it might be.

"Now, you're just guessing," she said accusingly. "Look, Mr. Steinberg, if the doctor just relied on guesswork, things would get loused up pretty fast around here." Oh why can't I control myself, she said to herself. Well, there goes the movie contract. "Why don't we get the rest of your measurements after you see the doctor?"

"Fine by me."

"Now, Saul," she said, returning to a more friendly tone, "I have to ask you a few questions that you might think are very personal but really aren't intended that way, so please don't be offended." As the nurse said this, she glanced up at the clock. "The doctor will be here in a jiffy, so let's get on with this information. Let's see now." She twirled the tip of the pencil on her tongue as she scanned the form. "Have you ever had hepatitis, stricture of the urethra, herpes, syphilis, gonorrhea, or...have you ever been bitten by a dog?"

"Bitten by a dog? Does that really matter? Well, no. I was scratched by a dog once."

"Scratched by a dog." She put the notation on the pad. "Now about the herpes and clap and stuff like that?"

"No!" Saul said emphatically. "Good heavens, no."

The nurse's attitude stiffened. She probably wouldn't have gotten the movie contract anyway and besides, his new movie company might fall flat on its face. "Mr. Steinberg, it really doesn't matter that much whether you answer these questions honestly or not as far as I'm concerned, because I want you to know, we have ways of finding out."

"I did answer honestly," Saul insisted. "And what do you mean you have ways of finding out? What sort of place is this, C.I.A. headquarters?" Saul's voice was growing louder.

"Now look, Mister Steinberg," the nurse whispered through clenched teeth, "I may just be a nurse here, but you are all of thirty-eight years old and you're trying to tell me you never even had herpes? And I suppose you never had syphilis?"

Saul stood up, on the verge of walking out. He leaned over, his face close to hers and whispered back, "Lady, I never had syphilis or herpes, and I don't care whether you believe me or not, but I'll tell you this, I can't think of anyone I'd rather not catch them from than you!"

Sandra saw that the patient was getting ready to walk out. I better calm him down a bit, she said to herself. After all, I want to hold onto this job until the right guy comes along. "Mr. Steinberg," she said in a calm even voice, "why don't you just sit down and relax a bit. Every business, as you must know, has its difficult moments. I bet you have some difficult moments in the movie world, don't you? By the way, I have a friend who would love to pick up a few bucks on the side. She has the kind of figure men pant over. You know, even a guy in your shape might get a little tingly over seeing her."

"What the devil do you mean by 'in my shape?' Look, I may be here to see the doc for his advice, but that doesn't mean I don't get tingly all the time!"

"Sorry, but wait a minute," Sandra exclaimed. "These movies of yours, they're not any of that dirty gay stuff are they?"

"No, they aren't."

"Good, because there's dirty, and there's dirty, if you know what I mean. Sort of like clean-dirty between men and women and the others that are real goddamn filthy dirty."

"Well, I hate to disappoint your girlfriend, but I don't make clean-dirty movies or dirty-dirty movies. My pix are on the level. Serious stuff. For example, right now I'm thinking of trying to re-create that majestic feeling of the great outdoors. The way it used to be in the early days of America. People don't spend hardly enough time out of doors any more. By the way, we're planning to start shooting in a month. We'll be up near Great Falls on the Potomac. If you get a chance, why not drop by? I will probably need some extras. And if your girlfriend is interested, bring her along too."

"The Potomac? You mean you're trying to put that filthy, dirty polluted river into a movie? Look, Mr. Steinberg, it's time to turn you over to the doctor, but let me say this: if you ever get sick of making a movie of that dirty river, and you want to get around to some clean dirty movies, give me a call."

As the nurse walked out, Saul looked up to see a smiling Dr. Doctor enter the examination room. The doctor gave Saul a warm handshake and inquired about the president's father. "His name is Harry, isn't it?"

"Yes, that's right. And he's fine, Saul replied. "I saw him just the other day."

"So you keep in close contact. Good! And by the by, how is the movie business, Mr. Steinberg? I overheard you discussing it with Sandra."

"To tell you the truth, I'd feel a lot more comfortable about it if I could get some real financial backing."

"Same here," the doctor said, with a trace of a hangdog look.
"It takes money to do things these days. Now, let's talk about you. Do you mind if I call you Saul?"

"Not at all, John."

"Good. Now let me tell you more about our program."

"Doc...I mean *John,* I'm really not interested in your program. I mainly came to get a referral."

"I see. But please be patient and listen anyway. You might just find it helpful. Our program isn't just for men who feel they have a penis-minum problem and would lead a happier life with a larger organ."

"That's what I meant when I said I wasn't interested in your program. I'm OK in that department, Doc."

"Really? Based on the information collected from Sandra on your chart, I would say you are not quite normal in that department. Let me be frank. I deduce from the data that your organ is somewhat smaller than average for a man of your size. But be that as it may, our program has a considerably broader focus than merely organ size. We also treat men who have...what shall I call it?...Ah yes, failing powers. Nurse Sandra's notes put you squarely in that category. And I see on the chart that you are apparently allergic to Viagra."

"But, Doc, I mean, John, I'm only thirty-eight. Maybe this is all temporary. I might be in a slump."

"Of course, we, any doctor that is, would have to do a lot of tests, but you may be in a steady, irreversible decline. It doesn't happen this early to many men, but it does happen."

"But how could a transplant help?"

"Obviously, the organ would be larger and thus more powerful. Let me explain: take an automobile engine for example. A larger engine is more powerful than a smaller one. Don't you agree?"

"Yes, I suppose so."

"Another example: wouldn't you say a larger lion is more powerful than a smaller one?"

"Yes, of course."

"So, there you have it. Now, as I said, until we've completed a series of tests, blood work, cardiac function, etc., I can only give you a conditional yes about the benefits in your case. But, if it is yes, as it happens, an opportunity has just arisen. A man incarcerated in Sing Sing Prison in New York, has received permission to donate and have his sentence reduced."

"Hope he wasn't a sex offender."

"Oh no. This man was just an armed robber. Held up a bank, a supermarket, stuff like that. Nothing disgusting."

Saul, growing increasingly anxious, tried to divert the discussion away from himself for the moment. "Doc, tell me about that old geezer I saw here a little while ago. Are you really able to arrange a transplant for an old guy like that? He must be all of eighty. Wouldn't you think that at his age, he'd be finished with sex?"

"I don't like to discuss one of my patients *with* a patient, but I think I can make an exception here. That man is actually eighty-four years old. He has been married four times. His last wife died a year ago. He claims he has fathered a total of twenty-two children. He wants someone less fortunate than himself to benefit from his God-given gift."

"Saul was astonished. "You mean he wants to be a *donor*?"

"Precisely. And now there's something I'd like to point out. If it turns out that you would benefit from the procedure, I can't give you a break on the operating room costs, but I can give you a substantial discount on the charge for my services."

"Why would you do that?"

"I would do it if you could provide some access to the president for my organization."

"Are you saying the president might need one of these?"

"No, no. I doubt it. I also feel a man in his position would hardly have time for sex, discounting of course, men like Kennedy and Clinton. What I need, Saul, is simply an endorsement of sorts from David Fishman. He might make even a casual remark that he knows of the procedure and knows someone who benefited from it. That someone might, in fact, be you. In this country, all it takes is a comment from the president to launch a new industry."

Saul got up to leave the doctor's office. "Well, Doc, I'll level with you. I don't expect to have any contact with the president until some day in the future when I see him at a family function, a Bar Mitzvah, perhaps. Even then, he would be surrounded by family and I might not be able to get a word in. But the president's father, Harry, is in a good position to plug your organization with his son."

"Perhaps you didn't know," the doctor said with a crestfallen look. "I've called him."

"Yes, Harry said you called, but he didn't tell me what happened."

Dr. Doctor looked down at the floor. He shook his head. He began pacing the floor in the small examination room. "Frankly, I'm almost ashamed to tell you what he said. It was very unfair. He called me a quack. He said I go around the country collecting private parts from people and pasting them on other people and if he had his way, he'd paste one on my face."

* * * * *

After Saul left the doctor's office, Sandra knocked softly on the door to the doctor's private office.

"Come in."

"Doctor, can I have a word with you?"

"Of course, Come in and sit down. Something troubling you?"

"Yes,. It's not personal. It has to do with the way you're advertising the practice."

Well, I must admit, I'm having a devil of a time getting the word out and obviously an even harder time keeping the office alive financially."

"I have a suggestion that might help."

The doctor leaned back in his swivel chair, toying with a letter opener that was hardly ever used since few letters were coming into the office. "Sandra, what do you suggest?"

"You have the receptionist out there pumping out letters one by one with little to show for it. It's time the practice moved into the modern age. We need to have a web site developed and promoted on the internet. That would instantly open up your program to the entire world. For example, I spent several years working as a nurse in the Orient and I know for a fact that Oriental men have a particular kind of sexual problem."

"Based on the statistics, with China having over a billion people, I really find that hard to believe."

"Yes, but from a woman's point of view, Oriental men don't provide much in the way of sexual satisfaction. And it's because of just what you've been talking about – the size of the penis."

"Sandra, are you suggesting that penis size is somewhat ethnically related?"

"Yes I am. Doctor, did you know that many Oriental Women pressure their husbands to have an operation performed...I don't know the technical name for it...but it has to do with an incision on the inner, underside portion of the penis. The result is a slightly longer organ. The women say that it helps, but not much."

The doctor was skeptical. "Has this become common practice?"

"Maybe not in China, but I know it is becoming common in Japan."

"But how would this help us financially?"

"Men would sign up on the internet, put down a deposit by credit card, and gain a position in a queue."

"You're speaking of recipients rather than donors obviously."

"Yes, of course."

"Well, how do we get this web site business started? I don't know anything about it."

"I have a friend who operates a small business. The company goes under the name REX Media. If you approve, I can contact them at rexchannel.com. They will design a web site for a very moderate cost. Then we arrange to have a host put the site on-line, again for a small cost. Believe me, Doctor, this could really turn things around. Of course, you would have to redouble your efforts to find donors. But the new financing would really help with that. And, if you don't mind my making a comment about your medical practice, what if you didn't replace an entire penis? What if you just extended one? Then, the donor would still have part of it left. And if the donor was 'well-endowed' he might be satisfied with something a bit more normal in size. What do you think?"

"It's really not a bad idea. I confess I had been thinking of entire replacement of the organ, but some men night be satisfied with less while others could have a bit more. What effect do you think this would have on women?"

"Well, Doctor, I happen to know that smaller women, more diminutive, shall we say, who are married to extremely well-endowed husbands, could be happy if the man were not quite so well-endowed."

As Sandra got up to leave the office, the doctor said, "Sandra, if we can pull all this off, I'm going to nominate you for sainthood."

13

Harry was growing impatient. Another red light. They were sitting there without any car in sight in either direction. "Why don't they use flashers at this time of the morning? At five-thirty in the morning, stopping for a red light on an empty street seems ridiculous. Saul, just drive through it. Ignore the damn thing. We're going to be late."

"I know you're anxious, Harry, but that's one thing I'm not going to do. Besides, this stop gives me a chance to take another bite out of my doughnut and maybe time for another sip of coffee."

Saul drove on when the light changed. He and Harry were heading down Connecticut Avenue toward the center of the city. Earlier, Saul had stopped by to pick up Harry at his apartment in Chevy Chase. As they approached Pennsylvania Avenue and Tenth Street, in northwest Washington, it was almost six A.M. "Pull over here, Saul. Like I said, they come by here a few minutes after six."

Saul parked at the curb, very close to the corner. Harry twisted around on the front seat of the car looking up the avenue in the direction of the White House to see if they were coming.

They waited. Harry fidgeted. They waited some more. "Maybe we got here too late. Maybe they came through before we got here. I told you to go through those red lights."

"Harry, I really don't think we got here late. You know what I think? He's either out of town on business or he's got a cold or something and doesn't feel like taking his bike out this morning. Besides, it's pretty chilly and damp out today."

"My son doesn't let the cold weather stop him. He loves biking in the cold. He says it is highly invigorating."

Ten minutes to seven. "Harry we're wasting our time. He never goes out riding this late."

"He did in New York. In New York, I don't mind telling you, he rode at any time of the day."

"But he's president now. He only has time to ride in the early morning. He's too busy to go out riding later in the day; besides the Secret Service would never allow him to go out in Washington traffic. It's the worst in the nation."

"Second worst. Los Angeles is first worst."

"OK, second worst. But I am sure we missed him. Let's go home. I need some more sleep."

* * * * *

It was five-thirty on the following morning. They were stopped at a light. Harry fidgeted as Saul sat quietly behind the wheel munching on his doughnut and sipping his coffee.

"Again, we'll be late like we were yesterday."

"Harry, we weren't late yesterday. He just didn't ride his bike, that's

93

all."

"Maybe you're right. But about this hunch of mine, I know I'm right. They're still after him, even though their first try failed. They didn't get him when they shot at his helicopter."

"You're right. The bazookas, or whatever they were, missed the target. The paper said they pooped out. Didn't even get near enough to hit the helicopters. What that tells me is that these guys aren't very competent."

"If I was an assassin," Harry added, "which I am not, I wouldn't use bazookas to go after helicopters, I'd sit right here and ambush him as he rode his bike down the avenue. That's my hunch. Doesn't it make sense?"

"Considering that whoever tried to do it with high tech failed, I agree it does make sense that they'd try something simpler, just as you say, Harry. But what can we do to protect him? He's surrounded by Secret Service. It's their job to protect him."

"How can they protect him when he rides so far out in front of the pack. I've seen the picture in the paper. They can't keep up with him."

The pair waited, parked on the corner of Pennsylvania Avenue and Tenth Street. The seven o'clock news came on the car radio. "Harry, another day, another miss. And this morning I know we got here early enough. We were here before six."

"You're right. Let's try again tomorrow morning."

* * * * *

Ten minutes to six on the following morning. Saul and Harry were parked on the corner of Tenth Street and Pennsylvania Avenue, just as they had been for the previous two mornings. Harry was twisted around on his seat looking up the avenue. They waited. Harry fidgeted. Saul finished his doughnut. He licked the powdered sugar off his fingers one-by-one. He finished his coffee and stuffed the mug under the seat.

Harry spied a group of bikers coming. "Saul, Saul," he said in a near shout, "here they come. Let's get going."

Saul immediately pulled the car partly out onto the avenue and as David Fishman went by on his bike, Saul whipped the car out behind the president and began trailing close behind him. The Secret Service men were almost half a block behind. Seeing the car, they tried to speed up. In a panic, they were pedaling like there was no tomorrow. And if the president was so much as injured, they knew that as far as their jobs were concerned, there would be no tomorrow.

David Fishman on his bike led the impromptu parade, followed by Saul and Harry in the car. Bringing up the rear, came the Secret Service. Twelve men pedaling so hard a cardiologist would have predicted at least three heart attacks among the men; a psychotherapist would have predicted at least two complete nervous breakdowns; and a urologist would have predicted one serious case of wet jockey shorts.

As the parade reached Fourth Street, a black sedan came roaring out of the street onto the avenue, heading directly at the president. Saul pressed on the accelerator and swung his car over aiming it directly at the other car. His intention was to smash into it if it was the only way to divert the other car. In the confusion, the president was able to maneuver his bike to avoid both cars and was last seen pumping along the avenue leaving everyone else in the dust.

The driver of the black sedan, distracted by Saul's car, and having missed his target, swerved to avoid the car carrying Saul and Harry. The black sedan continued across the intersection and roared down a cross street. General Ali Karasek, with Colonel Karam as a front seat passenger, careened along the street barely missing parked cars, and turned off into a small side street where the pair jumped out, abandoning the car. They clambered into a waiting van driven by the burly Hassar who let out a grunt as he gunned the van out of its parking space leaving a twenty-foot long patch on the street.

Saul, having prevented harm to the president, stopped his car and sat with his head down on the steering wheel, his heart pounding and his hands shaking in a palsied-like tremor.

Following a carefully laid plan in the event of such emergencies, four of the twelve Secret Service men followed David Fishman along Pennsylvania Ave, four swung off to follow the black sedan and the other four stopped to surround Saul's car. They approached the car, guns drawn. "Come out with your hands up!"

As Saul and Harry sheepishly stepped out of the car, the Secret Service slapped cuffs on each of them and ordered them to lean over the hood of the car. After frisking and finding no weapons, the agents started to push them into a police car that had just arrived on scene. They were informed they were under arrest.

Harry was sheepish no longer. He was livid. "You shmucks are arresting the wrong guys. Don't you realize, we saved his life. I'm the president's father."

"And I'm Julius Caesar," one of the agents said sarcastically.

"Wait a minute," another agent said. "I recognize him. I saw his picture in the paper. Yes, he is the president's father, by God."

An agent who identified himself as the senior agent-in-charge approached Harry. "Mr. Fishman, please accept our apologies. But tell us," he asked, pointing at Saul, "were you kidnapped by this guy? Is he the real assassin?"

"He's also a relative of the president," Harry explained. "He came down here with me. We were trying to do what we could to prevent someone from harming my son. What you should be doing is going after that other car. They're the real assassins."

"We have that covered. Four of our guys are after them. And we've called in the whirlybirds. Don't worry, we'll get them."

Just as the senior agent confidently predicted that the occupants of the black sedan would be apprehended, the four agents who had followed it, rode up on their bikes. One of the pursuing agents, still astride his bike, said, "They're gone. They got away in a van. Couldn't catch it and couldn't get a make on it.

But we checked out the car they were driving. It was stolen."

"But what about the van? Can't the choppers spot it?"

"Let me call and check. I see. Yes, I get it. Damn shame. A bummer." Turning to the senior agent, the agent on the bike said, "Well, they found the van. The D.C. police have checked it out."

"Great. Good work. But why did I hear you say 'bummer'?"

"Well, the van was also stolen and apparently after driving it a short distance, the suspects dumped it just like the black sedan, and must have gotten away in a third car. Nobody has any idea what the make is on the third vehicle."

The senior agent shook his head in disgust. He approached Harry. "Mr. Fishman and Mr...aah..."

"Steinberg."

"Yes, Steinberg. Did either of you get a good look at the occupants of the car?"

"Yes, of course," Harry said. "At least, I think so. They were two older women. A blonde and a redhead. They both had long hair and wore thick glasses. The driver looked to be on the heavy side but the one on the passenger side looked kind of thin. Don't you agree Saul?"

"Yes. That's a good description, but Harry, I can't be sure about something. I think there's something you left out."

"Something I left out?"

"Yes. One of them seemed to have a droopy black mustache."

Harry replied that at his age, his eyes weren't too good but he didn't remember seeing a mustache. "It looked to me like one of them was eating a chocolate doughnut."

"Harry, a chocolate doughnut is dark brown. What I saw was black."

"Is there any chance," Harry asked the senior agent, "if it might be just a simple case of two little old ladies running a red light while one of them was eating a doughnut?"

"I doubt it," the senior agent replied thoughtfully. "Little old ladies don't usually drive around in stolen cars...then dump the car for a stolen van...then dump the van for another car. No, I have to say this was a real attempt on your son's life. Well, anyway, Mr. Fishman, thanks for your help."

"What about the suspects?"

"Sorry to say they got away. Of course, we'll keep on the case. You can rest easy that we'll bird-dog it all the way, but I have to tell you we don't have much to go on. However, there's one thing I have to tell you. We won't need your help any more. We are going to do two things: first, we have to insist to your son that he change his route every day. We know he doesn't want to do that because he said he loves riding down Pennsylvania Avenue, but in cases like this we have the power to overrule him. Second, realizing that none of our agents can keep up with your son, we plan to have two limousines riding abreast of him. We'll have one on his left, the other on his right. Then the rest of the agents on bicycles can bring up the rear."

"Why don't you just let all the agents use motorcycles? That would make it easy for them to stay close and keep up with my son."

So They Went and Elected a Jewish President

"Mr. Fishman...Sir. Take my word for it, we've considered all the alternatives. We've already decided against motorcycles. Can you imagine the complaints we would receive if a dozen motorcycles roared through the city at six in the morning? People would think that Rolling Thunder, that gang of Vietnam vets, or Hell's Angels had come to town. Trust us. Let us do it our way."

Harry shrugged. He and Saul got back into Saul's car and they started driving home. "Well, anyway Saul, now you can go back to sleeping in as long as you want in the morning. But I'm convinced there are some people who are determined to hurt my son, and even kill him. Regardless of what the agent said, we have to stay on the alert. We need to keep a watch out for two little old ladies, thick glasses, one heavy set, one thin, one with long blonde hair, the other a redhead."

"What about the mustache?"

"Saul, I agree that what I saw was probably not a doughnut, but don't you know anything about criminals? That one probably shaved her mustache off by now."

*****

The newspapers and TV stations reported nothing about an attempted assassination. The only mention was a small item that an accident almost occurred on Pennsylvania Avenue during the president's morning bike ride when a woman in a speeding car with a woman passenger, apparently ran a red light.

Saul took a sip of his drink. "So Harry, how are you and Rose doing since you moved down to Washington?" Saul asked as he and Harry stood on the balcony of a penthouse suite of the Watergate apartment complex overlooking the Potomac River.

"We are doing OK. I saw you just the other day. I told you the same thing when you asked me then. I told you the week before and the week before that. Why do you keep asking?"

"Frankly, you don't seem to be very happy. Are you still worried about an assassination plot?"

"Of course, but what can I do about it? From what I read, there are over three million people in the greater Washington area. You could look forever for that blonde and redhead with the thick glasses. So my feeling now is to let the Secret Service handle the problem."

"Harry, on the bright side, the kind of life you have down here sure beats running that store on Long Island, doesn't it?"

"I wouldn't say that. I got a lot of satisfaction running my own business. I love my son, but down here I'm living in reflected glory. That's confidential, Saul. If Rose heard me kvetching, she'd raise hell. Another thing, since right after the November election when Rose and I moved down, we've had invitations coming in constantly. This party, that party, this embassy, that ambassador's home...Oy! Rose never turns down an invitation. I get tired thinking about it. I've already worn out one tuxedo. So we go to these parties and I stand around while they ask me about David. They talk about politics. They seem to think I can give them some inside information. I know little and care less about politics. And if I had inside information, I wouldn't tell them anyway."

"I don't mean to pry into your private life, Harry, but how can you earn a living just going to parties?"

"The money situation is good. I still have a lot of money left over from sale of the store. Added to that, Rose has been going on the lecture circuit. She got twenty-five thousand dollars for one lecture last week. Lecturing is apparently OK, but when I signed up to appear in a commercial for television, the White House put a stop to that. However, financially, we're doing very well. Saul, let's talk about your new company. Did the money I invested help out?"

"It was a godsend and I want to thank you. In fact, it got the company off the ground."

"How's the rest of the financing coming?"

"It's getting better all the time and I expect to make a killing tonight. Georgina Catheta let out the word that we would be here. Not so much about Sylvia and me, of course, but word that you and Rose, the president's parents would be here."

"So, how does that help?"

"Look Harry, in today's world it's access that counts. Anyone with access to the president has an inside track."

"All well and good, but speaking of access, have you seen him lately?"

"Well no. But these people don't know that."

"Saul, I hope you are successful but I hope you don't wind up promising something to investors that you can't deliver."

"Harry, access is vague. No one can pin it down. All I do is say maybe I can put in a word for them or their company or whatever their interests may be...logging, expanded oil drilling in the arctic, coal production, whatever. They understand that my efforts may not amount to much."

"I hate to be disagreeable, but logging in protected forests, expanded oil drilling in the arctic and increased coal production are not so good for the environment and you know how passionate David is about the environment."

"That's why these people need help."

"Are you in favor of destroying the environment?"

"Of course not. Harry, gimme a break. I need investors. They hear the word 'cousin of the president' and they pull out their checkbooks. I may have to beat them away with a stick. I promise little or nothing in return."

Harry tried to say something but Saul couldn't hear it because another plane was coming in low over the river, landing lights on, landing gear down, wingtip beacons flashing, preparing to land at Reagan National Airport. Harry waited for the plane to land. He spent a few moments in thought as he gazed across the river at the bright lights of Virginia on the opposite shore. "A mitzvah. I want you to do me a mitzvah."

"Sure, Harry. What?"

"It would be a big mitzvah if you kept my name out of this business. I gave you some startup money, but I want my name out of it. Please! I don't know anything about making movies. All I know is how to go to the movies, which incidentally, I don't have time for any more."

"It's a fascinating business. I'll have to bring you out to the set one of these days."

"Where is the set? You have a studio somewhere?"

"Not yet. So far we've been doing all the shooting outdoors. Right now we're up on the Potomac River. Up past Great Falls. Area called Seneca."

"And what do you do in this place called Seneca?"

"We're doing a remake of *Gone With The Wind*. And we're also working on a second picture."

"What do you call the remake: *Son of Gone With The Wind*?" Harry wore a grin as he made the comment. "And tell me, how can you make two pictures at once? Do you have two sets of actors?"

"No, just one set. Quentin Tarantino does it all the time. Harry, look at it this way. I can use the same actors and actresses and the same costumes in both movies. On top of that, I can use the same equipment and the same horses."

"Horses? How many horses?"

"I've collected over three hundred. I emptied every stable and farm in the area. Some of the scenes are pretty big. These films are epics, Harry."

"Tell me about the other plot. *Gone With The Wind* I already know."

"Well, they are somewhat similar. As you know, in *Gone With The*

Wind, the Union wins."

"Wait a minute, are you telling me that in your other movie, the South wins?"

"Not quite. They lose, but not as badly. Harry, I don't want to brag, but when I get finished, *Gone With The Wind* is going to look like a dumb soap opera by comparison."

"That may be, but I'm confused. Tell me, how do the actors know which picture they're in? Don't they get their lines mixed up?"

"Harry, I see you just don't understand. The dialogs are very similar, it's just the plots that are different."

"I know I don't understand. Don't try any more to explain, I still would not understand. But I'll come up and see for myself one of these days, maybe then I'll understand."

* * * * *

As Harry and Saul sipped their drinks on the balcony, Rose and Sylvia were in one of the party rooms. They were surrounded by admirers.

Georgina Catheta, Washington's leading socialite was complimenting Rose on being America's first mother.

"Thank you, Georgina," Rose replied, addressing the ladies around them, "and I know you mean well, but it makes me sound old. I wasn't the first. There were a lot of mothers in this country before me. Ha, ha!"

"And you, Sylvia...the president's first cousin."

"Georgina," Sylvia said demurring, "I'm just *one* of the president's first cousins. He has two other first cousins, which makes me one of three first cousins. And when you get to second cousins, and cousins once removed..."

"I see," Georgina replied, noticing that a few of the women surrounding them began to talk among themselves thus threatening to deprive Georgina and her principal guest of the limelight. If the conversation ever got around to third cousins or first cousins twice removed, her party would have made the next day's edition of *The Washington Post* as one of the dullest parties of the season.

Walking into the main party room, Georgina said in a loud voice: "Everyone. Please gather 'round. We're going to hear a few remarks from the country's first mother."

Rose moved to the center of the throng that had gathered in a circle, drinks in hand. Harry came in from the balcony and stood beside her. "Ladies and gentlemen," Rose said in opening, "I would like to make a few remarks. These are about my son, who I suppose you know is president and about his wife Lisa, who as you may know is first lady. To begin with, rumors to the contrary, the first lady is not pregnant. And despite what the *National Enquirer* wrote recently, I'm not pregnant either. Ha, ha! Maybe next week," Rose said jokingly as she put an arm around Harry's shoulder. Harry looked like he had been shot between the eyes as people in the crowd chuckled, and a few men began poking one another with their elbows.

So They Went and Elected a Jewish President

"I can now divulge another secret," Rose went on. "My son is getting a dog. I suppose the papers will call it 'the first dog,' although some people wonder about that since the country already seems to be filled with dogs. My son, David, says the White House is pretty empty without man's best friend. Of course, the first lady would take issue with that. My son also told me that one of these days he's going to be a surprise guest at one of Georgina's wonderful parties."

The announcement was followed by a round of polite applause as Georgina put on a smile that was so wide it caused tiny cracks in the corners of her lips.

"Now," Rose continued, "I would like to introduce my nephew, Saul Steinberg who is an up-and-coming movie producer."

The crowd hushed as Saul walked over and stood next to Rose and Georgina. The ladies in the crowd smiled at the tall handsome man who for the occasion had tied a colorful silk scarf around his neck held in place with a gold stickpin embossed with the letters 'SP'— all of the trademarks, so he thought, of his new profession. "Thank you, Aunt Rose. And thank you, Georgina, for inviting my wife and me to this splendid party. The letters on my stickpin here refer to my company, SP, Steinberg Productions. Yes, folks I'm beginning a movie. It's going to be a blockbuster. I can now announce that we're doing a remake of *Gone With The Wind*."

At the mention of the classic, a buzz went through the crowd.
A man in the back said, "By heavens, you're really taking on a big one! By the way, who's your director?"

"I am," Saul answered modestly.

"And who wrote the new screenplay?"

"Me, again," Saul answered.

"Wow! Producer, writer, director. How many movies have you made thus far, Mr. Steinberg?"

"None so far, but there's one thing I can say, I'm off to a fresh start. And I feel that enthusiasm is the most important thing and I've got a lot of that."

"What about money? Have you got any of that?"

"I have some funding," Saul replied guardedly. "Yes, we're funded. Not completely, of course. In fact, we're still looking for a few investors. Not many, just a few."

"Who's the 'we'?"

"Oh, me and the president's father, Harry, here."

Harry scowled, but not wanting to hurt Saul's chances, he quickly changed his expression to a smile. So much for that mitzvah, he said to himself.

At the mention of the president's father, a small circle of men gathered around Saul and Harry. The remainder of the guests began to drift away.

One balding, heavy-set man said: "Put me down for five hundred thousand. On second thought, make it two million."

And who do you represent?" Saul asked.

"I'm president of Midwest Coal and Gas."

101

Another man, not to be outdone said: "Put me down for five million."

"And who are you with?" Saul inquired as he advanced to shake the man's hand.

"I'm CEO of Western States Logging Company."

"I see," Saul replied, while Harry, moving up next to him, was so angry he was ready to kick Saul in the shins.

After several more substantial offers, Saul said: "Now gentlemen, I hope your investments are meant strictly as investments in a venture that holds real promise. If I thought you expected me to lobby the president on your behalf, I'd have to refuse your offers."

"We don't expect *you* to do it," one of the men said, "but we were hoping the president's father would say a few kind words to his son. What about it, Mr. Fishman?"

Harry tried to stay calm. He managed to keep smiling. "My son and I never talk politics or business. We talk only of family things: How's the wife? How did you like last Friday's shabbat dinner? Did you hear about my brother Matthew's heart condition? What kind of a dog are you going to get? What are you going to name the first dog? Stuff like that."

Despite Harry's apparent refusal to lobby on their behalf, several of the men kept their offers alive with Saul. They knew there was another possible route to the president. If Saul would talk to his wife, Sylvia, the president's first cousin, and Sylvia would talk to her aunt, Rose, the first mother, and Rose would talk to her son, perhaps the first son, when hearing it from the first mother, would pass the word back down to the first cousin-in-law, Saul, indicating that the White House was willing to loosen up a bit.

After all, as Saul and everyone else in these games know, access is everything.

* * * * *

"Places everybody. Quiet on the set. Action!"

"Saul, I don't mind telling you I'm a little nervous," Harry said as he looked down to the ground from almost twenty feet up in the director's motorized chair. "And this up-down, up-down, swinging around, I feel like I'm at an amusement park."

The scene was just above Seneca on the Potomac River where in a secluded area, the river narrows into two channels with a small wooded island in between.

"You'll get used to the movement, Harry," Saul said. "We can't stop now. This is one of our big scenes. The weather is perfect. Perfect spring day. We've got cameras rolling all over."

"I should know. I keep getting bumped on the head from the camera rolling right behind us."

"Harry, try to ignore it. Look over there, up the river about a coupla hundred yards. See all those horses and riders? That's part of General Lee's cavalry. They're trying to escape the Union Army by crossing the river."

"Where's Scarlett O'Hara?"

"She's not in this scene. She's only in the scenes we will shoot in the studio. You know, fancy dress balls and all that."

"You mean when you get a studio."

"Right."

"Saul, all this looks complicated. How do you keep it all under control?"

"Well, it isn't easy. I have my power megaphone right here and a cell phone to those far-off assistant directors on the set."

"How many horses did you say you have?"

"Three hundred in this scene plus eight wagons, and I managed to get fourteen cannons. See them up there being towed into the river? But, Harry, please, no more questions right now." Then, in a booming voice, Saul yelled: "John, dammit, can't you see some of those cannons are sinking in the river mud?" In an aside to Harry: "Well, I suppose it can't be helped. We'll have to dig them out later. We'll just play it as one of the losses of the retreat. After all, Lee did lose a lot of stuff in his rush to get across the river."

Harry was somewhat startled when the Union Army arrived and the real shooting began. Bullets seemed to be whizzing everywhere. It brought him abruptly back to his days in the Navy, off the coast of Korea. "Saul, this is like a real war."

"Not quite, they're using blanks and some rubber bullets to ping here and there when they hit the dirt. It's all for effect."

"I'm glad they're rubber, because one of them just hit me in the leg. Does this get any worse?"

"Just hang in there, Harry. After awhile, you'll be comfortable with the action."

"That may be, but I never found a way to get comfortable with being injured."

"OK. Camera three, in for a tight shot. Tighter, dammit, tighter!" Saul screamed.

"Saul, tell me. Just one question please. Are the audiences going to like the movie when they hear you yelling like that?"

"They won't hear any of this. We put the sound in later."

"So, this part is like a silent movie? A war going on in silence. I just don't understand."

"I'll explain it all later." Then, in a shout that would have toppled the Washington Monument, Saul yelled: "Get those guys in the business suits out of there! I don't give a rat's ass if they are investors. You can't have pinstripes in the middle of a Civil War battle scene."

"How do they all get across the river?" asked Harry.

"The river's real shallow here. Only a coupla feet deep. Oh, shit. Another wagon went over in the mud. And it looks like it broke up. The farmer who loaned us some wagons is gonna be mad as hell. Well, I'll just have to find a way to replace it. Now you see how tough this business is? And do you see why it takes a boatload of money?"

"I'm beginning to understand. I bet you used up the money I invested in almost an hour of shooting."

"Mind you, I'm not complaining, Harry, but we used up the money you invested in about sixty seconds of shooting."

* * * * *

Later, down on the ground, Saul and Harry walked over to a beautiful young woman standing nearby with a cup of coffee in her hand. She was wearing high heels, a low cut blouse and a mini-skirt that seemed to cover the part of her body that came to about one inch below her curvy tochis.

"Harry, you remember Dr. Doctor, don't you?"

"How could I forget?" Harry said as he felt a tiny tingle in his shorts.

"This is his nurse, Sandra. We recruited her to play the part of Scarlett O'Hara. Sandra, this is Harry Fishman, the president's father."

"Ooh," Sandra said in her most fetching voice. "Pleased to meet you. Could you arrange to have me sing Happy Birthday to your son at his next birthday party?"

"I'll try," Harry said. But inwardly, he couldn't help thinking that his son was no Jack Kennedy and this woman was no Marilyn Monroe, although when he took another look at her figure, and saw a few parts he had overlooked, he began to change his mind.

As the pair left Sandra and walked over to Saul's trailer, Harry was puzzled: "Why do you have a star on the door? You're the director, not the star."

"Well, Harry, in this business you have to stay flexible. I haven't been able to find the right guy to play Rhett Butler and I may have to do it myself."

"Be careful there, Saul. You certainly have the looks for the role but that New York accent might not go over too good."

"If it comes to that, I'll get a speech coach."

The two men entered the trailer. Saul poured Harry a cup of coffee. They sat looking out the window. Harry pointed to Sandra who was standing talking to a group of male extras.

"So, tell me, why do you have that nurse who looks like a hooker playing the part of Scarlett O'Hara? From what I remember, Scarlett was a refined southern belle. If it was up to me I'd sooner see someone with real beauty like your wife Sylvia in the part. Remember, Sylvia was a big hit in her college drama department."

"Thanks for the compliment, but there's no way Sylvia is going to be in this picture."

"Investors would think it was nepotism?"

"No. It has to do with the nude scenes."

"Wait a minute," Harry said as he as he stirred his coffee. "I don't remember any nude scenes in *Gone With The Wind*."

"You're right, there weren't any. But remember, this picture is a modern day remake and today's audiences insist on at least one nude scene. And there's no way I'm going to let my wife prance around naked while these clowns are ogling her."

There was a knock on the trailer door. When Saul opened it, he saw none other than General Robert E. Lee in full dress uniform. The general had a worried look on his face. "Come in general. What seems to be the problem."

"Saul, maybe you haven't noticed it but we've had heavy spring rains and the river is deeper than we thought. The horses can't walk across."

"So? Horses can swim. Let them swim across."

"But it's the current. If they were able to walk they'd be able to resist the current, but swimming, they're winding up all over the place. In the last take, thirty horses got swept downstream but maybe you didn't notice."

"No, I didn't. I was busy directing the Union Army. You're the damned general of the South's army. It's up to you to get your men across the river."

"In case you forget, Saul, I'm an actor, I was never in the army. And there's another problem. A big one. The cast is thoroughly confused about which picture you're making right now. You know, it's kind of nice to know what the hell picture you're supposed to be acting in."

"That's for me to worry about. I'll take care of all that in the editing. Just read your lines, that's all I'm asking. This is the third time you've complained today."

"Well, I'm not going to complain any more because I quit and if you try to hold me to that contract, I'll sue your ass off."

With that, General Robert E. Lee stripped off his sword belt and threw it on the floor. As he strode angrily away from the trailer, he scaled his hat into the river, and shouted to his troops: "Stand at ease, Men, the Civil War is temporarily on hold."

Harry was puzzled. "Saul, you're in the middle of shooting. How could you let him get away?"

"Harry, when you learn more about this business, you'll see that General Robert E. Lee's are a dime a dozen."

15

General Ali Karasek drove along Pennsylvania Avenue approaching Fifteenth Street. He was in a lighthearted mood due to two things that pleased him: first, that he was one block away from the man they intended to kill. He well knew how important it was to pinpoint the target. No need to search through dozens of cities and multitudes of people to find the victim. This victim lived right there a block away, and would continue to be there for four years or until his demise, whichever came sooner. 'Sooner' was much preferred to Ali's way of thinking.

The second thing that pleased him was the fact that the young man was right on time. There he was, standing on the street corner. As the general pulled the car over to the curb, he gave a wave of recognition to the young man. "Good morning, Abu. Get in."

The young man slid into the passenger seat and closed the car door. The two men shook hands. The general studied his passenger. He noted that the young man was dressed like a student: somewhat worn blue-jeans, loafers, and an athletic jacket over a woolen sweater. The young Arab's black hair was tousled. His thin angular face displayed a pleasant, although not handsome countenance. The centerpiece, of course was a good solid Arab nose. For a Palestinian, he had an unusually strong athletic build. Karasek's file indicated that Abu Aram worked out regularly in the gym.

"How are things going at the university?"

"Fine. It's an easy school."

"What university are you attending? Georgetown? George Washington?"

"No, you guys don't pay near enough tuition for those places. I'm at UDC, the University of the District of Columbia. It's subsidized by the city, so it's very cheap."

"You complain about the tuition money not being enough for an expensive private school, but I am told you drive a Mercedes, eat at fancy restaurants, and spend a lot of money on the ladies."

"I scrimp in other ways so I can have a few luxuries."

"In any case, it is now payback time."

"What does that mean?"

"It means, you have to go to work. We have an assignment for you."

"Do I have to drop out of school?"

"No. This is parttime. We want you to remain in school as you take on the new assignment."

"How am I supposed to keep up with my studies if I have to work parttime as well?"

"You will find a way. Besides, this assignment should be much to your liking."

Abu sat back, looking out the window at the Washington scene as Karasek turned at the corner and drove up Fifteenth Street.

"Where are we going?"

"North to Silver Spring. I want to show you an apartment."

So They Went and Elected a Jewish President

Abu twisted around in his seat to face the general. "If you think I'm going to live in Silver Spring and drive downtown to school every morning through that traffic mess, you're crazy."

"The apartment is not yours. It holds some Jewish people you are going to meet."

"Oh no! I know you're part Jewish, my general, but you're not bringing me into some circle of Jewish friends. By Allah, I both dislike and distrust them. They are trying to take Jerusalem away from my people."

"These are American Jews and they are not my friends, but they will play an important part in my plan."

"Just give it to me straight. What do I have to do?"

"Only a year in America and already you sound like an American teenager."

"I'm not a teenager. I'm twenty-one."

"You don't have to tell me about yourself. We know all about you. I knew you were at UDC. I even know your grades. We have a two-inch thick file on you, young man."

"Then why did you ask me what school I was going to?"

"Your file says you bitch about everything. I simply wanted to see if it was true. And it is true."

As the car pulled up across the street from a luxury apartment house in Silver Spring, General Karasek turned the motor off. "This is the place. They live in that apartment house over there."

"So, who?"

"Relatives of the new president. A family named Steinberg. Where you come in, Abu, involves one of their nieces who has just arrived in town. She is staying with them. Your assignment is to get to know her, start dating her, keeping your ears open all the while. We want you to find out where the president is going, when he is going, how he is traveling...car, helicopter, Air Force One, etc. His relatives will know. They will talk about it over lunch, over dinner. You will be listening. You will tell us. The camel's ears are tuned to the music of the desert breeze. It is as simple as that."

"Except for one thing. How do I get to meet the niece? And how do you expect me to start dating a woman I've never seen? What if she's a real dog? Why do I have to put up with that?"

"I think you will put up with it. Besides, this promises to be a pleasant assignment for you."

"How come?"

"The young woman named, Marsha, is very good-looking and has a forty-two inch bust. Admittedly, she is a bit high strung and can be difficult to deal with at times, but I am sure you can woo her and gain her confidence."

"Frankly, General Karasek, I find this hard to believe. She's a Jew, I'm a Palestinian."

"You are about to become a Jew."

On hearing that, Abu almost jumped out of the seat. "How in the name of Allah am I going to become a Jew?"

107

"Think about it, my young friend. If you were standing near the Western Wall in Jerusalem and two men passed by, both in identical dress, could you tell that one was a Jew, the other a Palestinian?"

"Well...the skullcap, the yarmulke."

"Without the yarmulke. You're hesitating because you know I am right. You people have lived side by side for thousands of years walking the same streets, living under the same sun. The only things that set you apart are your beliefs, your habits. So, to infiltrate the Steinberg family, you will only need to wear a yarmulke when you see them; you will make continual references to the Hebrew Bible, to the Torah."

"Allah forgive me, but yes, I can wear a yarmulke, but I don't know anything about Judaism. What if they question me?"

"Start taking a course."

"Hey, UDC has African-American studies but they haven't got any courses in Judaism."

"Then get some books. Go to synagogues. Pick up the phrases. We are not trying to turn you into a rabbi. All we need is the superficial appearance of Judaism. You do not have to eat kosher food. We know the deli they eat at. They do not eat kosher. All you have to do is wear a yarmulke, go to the synagogue, speak a few Jewish or Yiddish words now and then. The High Holy Days are another matter, I agree. They could be difficult, but we will be finished long before then."

"Look, general, all my friends at school know I'm not Jewish. How do I handle that?"

"At the university you are Abu Aram, as always. In Silver Spring with the Steinbergs you are Izzy. Let us call you Izzy Weinstein. It has a nice ring to it, don't you think?"

"What if I don't agree to take this assignment?"

"There is no doubt in my mind that you will take it."

"General, may I remind you of an ancient Arabian proverb?"

"Which one? There are thousands of them."

"Simply this one: 'You can lead a camel to the pool at the oasis but you cannot force him to slake his thirst.'"

"If we have to put one of your feet in scalding hot water and the other in a pail of crushed ice, I can assure you, you will slake your thirst."

* * * * *

Marsha, standing in front of the mirror in her Aunt Sylvia and Uncle Saul's bathroom, studied her face. She tried on the black wig. She thought it looked appropriate to wear to the synagogue for the Sabbath. But like most wigs, she thought it looked a little too smooth, so she ran her fingers through it to give it a more natural, slightly windblown look. As always, she applied her lipstick with a tiny brush and skillfully outlined her lips with another even smaller brush. Mascara, eyeliner and shadow completed her ritual. She studied the result in the mirror. She had done better on other occasions but she was running out of time and it would have to do.

Marsha well knew her effect on men and, in a way, enjoyed the stares, double-takes and whistles. On the other hand, she often thought that having an appearance like hers led to a great deal of uncertainty about people, men, in particular. She felt it was similar to the problem wealthy people must face: you never knew whether people were interested in you...or your treasure.

After her brief visit to Washington for the Inauguration, she had gone back to New York with a head full of dreams. Now that a close cousin of hers was president of the United States, if she moved to Washington, a whole new world would open up for her. Wouldn't she have a golden opportunity to meet handsome diplomats at lavish state dinners at the White House? And hadn't she told just about everyone that she might even get a job at the White House? Despite the new president's announced stand against nepotism, Marsha, thinking it applied to everyone else in the family except her, thought she might be able to wheedle her way in. When quizzed by her friends, she readily admitted that she hated paperwork and couldn't stand sitting at a computer terminal all day. After she made these admissions, people wondered what was left to do at the White House other than clean up after the president's new dog.

To say that Marsha's mother, Rachel, was angry when her daughter dropped out of N.Y.U. after two-and-a-half years to go to Washington, proved to be an understatement for the record books. Rachel's anger reached heights heretofore unscaled by some of the greatest mountain climbers. But the outbursts served only to convince Marsha that it was time to leave New York and strike out on her own.

When Marsha announced her plan to her boyfriend, she had even suggested he might come along. But he told her he was perfectly happy working as a ticket agent at Penn Station, and would never, ever leave the center of the universe: New York City. "Washington, D.C. may be a wonderful place to visit," he had said, "but who would ever want to live there?" So, they broke up and she moved down alone to occupy Sylvia and Saul's spare bedroom.

* * * * *

Abu Aram, alias Izzy Weinstein, stood near the front door of the Silver Spring apartment house. He occasionally glanced at a snapshot of a very good-looking young woman who had a forty-two inch bust. After studying the photograph, he slipped it back into the pocket of his short black leather jacket. It was the Sabbath and he was wearing the black yarmulke, the one with the delicate white embroidered border. No blue jeans today. His off-white cotton slacks were neatly pressed, the cuffs draped with a slight break over his dress black buckle boots. His black, normally tousled hair looked as if it had briefly been visited by a comb.

He knew she walked to the synagogue for Sabbath services. It was a short four block walk. He hoped today she would be alone.

Ten minutes to nine. If she didn't come out soon, she would be late. Maybe, he thought, she wasn't going to synagogue today. General Karasek told him she had only arrived in Washington several weeks before. The general also said that he, Abu, alias Izzy, would have an excellent opportunity because she had just broken up with her boyfriend.

Three minutes to nine. Izzy was thinking: I drive all the way out here from downtown, miss a Saturday morning class, and for what? She's probably turning over in bed for another fifty-seven winks as the Americans call it.

As he turned to leave, Izzy saw a figure coming through the lobby of the apartment. It was her! It was Marsha. The young woman hustled through the lobby, forty-two inch bust jouncing a bit under her jacket; then out the front door she came and began walking quickly down the street.

"Hey, goodlookin' whatcha' got cookin'?" he said as he started trailing after her.

She glanced back over her shoulder at the young man as she walked. She did not slow her pace. "Good grief, I haven't heard that opening line in years. Where did you dig it up? Is there a cemetery around here somewhere?"

"I suppose I should have said, 'Sholom.' Going to the synagogue? Mind if I tag along?"

"How did you know where I was going? Have you been spying on me?"

"No, but I was at the synagogue last Saturday. I saw you there and then I saw you come back here to your apartment. I was too shy to talk to you. But now I would really like to tag along with you, if it's all right."

"It's a free country. Only keep your distance. I don't like having to punch out some jerk just before I'm going to pray."

They walked the four blocks in silence. Izzy struggled to keep up with Marsha's long-legged, high-heeled, energetic stride.

During the service, they sat on opposite sides of the sanctuary. After the service, during the Oneg Shabbat in the room next to the sanctuary, Izzy walked over to Marsha as she stood alone with a cup of coffee in one hand, cradling a half-bagel covered with cream cheese and a thin slice of salmon in the other.

"Hi. I hope I didn't sound too fresh outside your apartment house. I was walking by and thought I recognized you from last week at the synagogue."

"You seem to have a foreign accent, and I wouldn't be surprised if you're not American, but where did you pick up those corny opening lines, hanging around Times Square in New York?"

"Sorry, but that's all I could think of. I wanted to meet you. Yes, you're right. I am a foreigner; I'm an Israeli... Jerusalem. My name is Isador. They call me Izzy."

Marsha's attitude softened. Maybe he isn't such a jerk, after all. Maybe he just doesn't know how you pick up a woman in the good old U.S. of A.

They talked for awhile. He told her of his early upbringing on a kibbutz; all about daily life in Jerusalem; about his desire for an American education; how he was studying at George Washington University. He thought the little white lie would help his image. Girls usually wore a smirk when you told them you were studying at U.D.C. They always asked: "Why are you going to the city school? Are you poor or something?"

"My, G.W.! An expensive school and I bet they don't give scholarships to foreigners, so you must have money. How did you get out here to Silver Spring? You come on Metro, or have you got a car hidden somewhere?"

"It's parked a few blocks away. I bought it soon after I got to Washington. I wanted a Porsche but was afraid it would be stolen or I would be carjacked, so I settled on a Mercedes. They are less conspicuous."

Marsha was curious. "How come you drive all the way out here to Silver Spring to attend this synagogue? They have dozens in Washington."

"I know, but I like to try new things. I've been to just about every one in the city."

This guy's really into religion, Marsha said to herself. More so than myself. He sounds pretty interesting, but I don't want to spend my life discussing passages from the Torah. "Tell me more about Israel."

"I will if you will have dinner with me. Perhaps the Four Seasons, or maybe you would prefer one of the seafood restaurants on the waterfront. And we could walk around and look at the boats."

"Ooh, too cold for that. Why don't we settle on the Four Seasons."

"Good. Pick you up at seven tonight."

Marsha was puzzled. "Aren't you even going to ask my name? How do you know who you have a date with?"

"Oh, of course..."

"It's Marsha. I'm staying with my aunt and uncle, the Steinbergs. Apartment ten-fifteen."

* * * * *

After dropping Marsha off at the street entrance to her apartment house, Izzy couldn't help thinking what a pleasant assignment Karasek had given him. It would be a pain driving out to Silver Spring, but well worth it. He wondered if he was falling in love. He knew from past experience that he was good at falling in love. It only took about fifteen minutes after meeting a beautiful woman to discover he was giddily descending the precipitous, slippery slope of love. The slide down was too exhilarating for words; it was the lonely struggle back up that was enormously difficult. It usually produced a reaction described as 'never again,' but by Allah, when the next beautiful woman came along...

111

16

The excursion boat plowed through the choppy waters of the Potomac River steaming south to Mount Vernon. Under gray overcast skies, and in the midst of early spring weather that was still somewhat raw, the first trip of the new excursion season was launched with an almost empty boat. Later in the season it would be filled with screaming schoolchildren accompanied by teachers and parents who would try in vain to keep them from lambasting one another in food fights, from spilling soft drinks, from dropping mustard-smeared hot dog buns on the decks, and from roughhousing that produced an epidemic of skinned knees and bloody noses. But today, all was serene on the almost empty steamer.

The steady throb of the engines pulsed through the soles of his feet as General Ali Karasek stood leaning against the railing on the top deck watching the shoreline go by. Colonel Zumar Karam and the burly Hassar stood nearby. Of the three men, Hassar was the only one fat enough not to be uncomfortable in the damp chilly air.

Colonel Karam pointed to the line of tall green pines on the bank of the river. "There is a beauty in this country," he remarked thoughtfully. "There is green everywhere. It is quite pleasant to look at. In my homeland, there is only the color of sand. The air here has a moist fresh scent. It is not filled with the scent of fresh camel dung."

"Do not get too attached to it," Karasek warned, flipping his cigarette into the water. "I know you both think my plans are long drawn out, but even so, we are not going to be here that much longer. And, of course, after the job is done, we can never come back. Not for many years anyway."

The colonel and the Libyan went below decks to get some coffee and a sandwich as Karasek strolled up to the bow by himself. He wasn't hungry and he wanted to do a little thinking. Their first attempt, hastily put together with the Libyan missiles in the woods north of Washington, had failed miserably. It pained him just thinking about it. The intelligence about the president's helicopters that were supposed to fly to Camp David that day proved to be quite reliable. It was intelligence of the highest quality. It came from the American newspapers. A completely free country is a wonderful thing for an assassin, he thought. If one reads the papers carefully, one can tell the president's destination, when he will arrive and how long he will stay.

The thing that bothered him deeply however, was the failure of the Libyan missiles. How could that have happened? Why was he subjected to the incompetence of others? Untested in cold weather, or maybe due to obsolescence, the shoulder-fired missiles were completely incapable of overcoming the defenses of the president's helicopters. It was an embarrassment. Surely, colleagues in the Middle East would be snickering. It could affect his future assignments. And Karasek was well aware that the Secret Service was alerted, perhaps even in a crisis mode after the incident. Now they knew that someone was after Fishman in earnest.

A short time later, however, Karasek could hardly believe his good luck when the newspapers reported that the president rode his bike along

So They Went and Elected a Jewish President

Pennsylvania Avenue at about six A.M. each morning. The papers even mentioned that he occasionally zoomed ahead of the accompanying Secret Service agents as if they were engaging in a bike race. If so, it would be an absurdly easy hit.

But the second attack also failed because of a pure accident of fate. Karasek and his cohorts knew they had put the plan together hastily, but it was a simple operation requiring little planning: two stolen cars plus a stolen van, all located for quick transfer and getaway; wigs as disguises; ladies' dresses; thick glasses; everything needed.

He remembered that they had waited in the mornings for over a week, posing as two little old ladies in a parked car sitting quietly and talking, looking as if they were waiting to pick up a carpool member before going to a government office for an early start on the workday. The colonel, of course, had fidgeted on the front passenger seat as usual and fiddled with his droopy black mustache, the only thing that on close inspection might have given them away. In spite of Karasek's orders, he had refused to shave it off. Meanwhile, Hassar had been stationed several blocks away in the van. They were ready.

Then, for some unknown reason, the president skipped his daily ride for several days. One of the curses of this business, Karasek thought, was the waiting around. Hours and hours of waiting seemingly to no purpose. But finally, the president came. It was perfect. He had separated from his security team. He was riding almost a block ahead of the nearest agent. Perfect, except for that accursed car. Old and somewhat battered, it could not have been a government car moving to intercept them. Where did it come from? How did it wind up between the president and his car? Why did that crazy driver swerve? Was he drunk at six in the morning?

As General Karasek strolled the top deck, recounting these unfortunate events to himself, Colonel Karam and Hassar rejoined him. The three men walked to the center of the deck and took seats on a damp bench. The colonel looked around nervously. He saw they were still all alone on the top deck. "What happens next?" he asked.

"I have set in motion a plan to infiltrate the Fishman family. We need better intelligence than we have been getting from the newspapers. Too many things can go wrong. We have to find some event that Fishman is certain to attend. Perhaps some unavoidable family occasion. Perhaps a Bar Mitzvah or a Bas Mitzvah, or a birthday party for one of his parents. Something along those lines."

"How," the colonel asked, "do you plan to infiltrate the family? No one of us can do it. Who do you have in mind?"

"I have already put the plan in operation. The operative is a young man who has been undercover here for a year. He poses as a student at a local university. His name is Abu. He is from Jerusalem. A Palestinian. That's all you have to know about him."

"But how does he infiltrate the family? A Palestinian infiltrates a Jewish family? Ali, you are out of your mind," the colonel said as his fidgeting almost took on the dimensions of a tremor.

113

"Calm down. You have become what the Americans refer to as a 'Nervous Nellie'."

"After two attempts and two failures, the danger grows."

"I know that, but now with the young man doing his infiltrating we can take a back seat for awhile. Of course, he is being employed only for intelligence. We...you Zumar, and you Hassar...and I...will do the actual killing. I would not deprive you of the splendid opportunity to become heroes in your homelands."

"Again how?" asked the usually silent Hassar, who when he suddenly spoke suprised both of his cohorts. It was like listening to a foghorn coming from the bridge of the steamer.

"Simple. Abu is posing as a Jew. He has already made the acquaintance of a young woman in the family. They go to the synagogue together. Whatever else they do together, I don't know and don't care to know."

"Is she beautiful?" The colonel was curious.

"She is not only beautiful, she has an awe-inspiring forty-two inch bust."

Both Colonel Karam and Hassar smiled. They agreed that Abu was indeed a lucky man. "But," the colonel asked, "what if he falls in love with her? Will he still give us reliable intelligence?"

"Yes. I am quite sure of that. When one foot is in a pot of scalding water and the other in a bucket of crushed ice, love seems to fade away and the information gleaned is always reliable."

Both Colonel Karam and Hassar agreed that the plan had merit, but the colonel was disturbed. He got up and walked over to the railing. He leaned over slightly to look at the water, then straightened up, grasping the top railing and bracing his arms straight against it. He stared at the far shoreline during a long silence. Suddenly, he wheeled around and walked back to the other men. He stood staring down at Karasek. "So what the devil do we do while this young man romances the girl? And after he gets to know the family, how long do we wait for the information we need? By the beard of Mohammed, Ali, this could take months and months."

Karasek lit another cigarette. He exhaled a stream of smoke. He was unperturbed. Time and again he had seen his friend, Zumar go through these petulant outbursts. Karasek smiled. He was determined to see this business through calmly. "What do we do? I'll tell you. We relax and enjoy ourselves! After all, do we have to be busy all the time, my nervous friend? If that's the way you think, you have chosen poorly your line of work. You know as well as I that espionage is either feast or famine. Months of boredom followed by a few moments of action, excitement and stark terror."

After stepping off the boat at Mount Vernon, the three men strolled across the wide green lawn. They admired the graceful white columns on the front portico of the first American president's home. And, after touring the palatial residence, they stood in silence at the graves of George and Martha.

By this time, the colonel had calmed down, reconciling himself to a long wait before the assassination. When you're dealing with a tortoise like Ali, he thought, what else can you do? Through the black wrought-iron bars of the mausoleum he stared at the white stone sarcophagus of George Washington. "What did he die of? Was he assassinated?"

"No, on the contrary," Karasek replied, "he died of something very rare...rare I mean as regards great revolutionary leaders. He died a natural death."

After touring the grounds, the men boarded the boat for the return trip to Washington. Hassar, normally a taciturn killer, was unusually loquacious on the cruise back: "If we are to kill him at a family event, I would like to be a Jewish waiter. I don't think Allah would mind if I wore a yarmulke for a few hours, considering that this is such a noble deed. I would kill him with poisoned Jewish food. It all tastes like poison anyway."

"I must disagree," Karasek interjected. "I find kugel, blintzes, kosher hot dogs, beef brisket, and many other Jewish foods, all very tasty."

"That's because you are half-Jewish," the colonel commented. "But in any case, poison is the weapon of women. I favor the pistol."

"The pistol is out," Karasek said bluntly. "Too much security around. We'd never get away. There may be something to what our Libyan friend is saying. Poison is difficult to trace. We could be far away by the time anyone noticed it or could find out where it came from. If it was slow acting, he might not die for hours."

Hassar beamed. For once, someone was listening to his suggestions, even though he was aware that he rarely made any suggestions. "I know," he said, "that Jews frequently eat bagels with cream cheese. I have heard of an explosive cream cheese. In fact, I think I can get some if we decided to use it. And if he takes a big bite...zap...off with the head."

Karasek looked over at Hassar. "What's this about explosive cream cheese? A big bite you say? What if on the other hand, he takes only a small bite? Listen, you idiot, we are trying to send Fishman to the undertaker...not to the dentist! But I have to admit that some type of poisoned food is worth considering. In the Middle East, a taster nibbles on the food before the Sultan eats any, but I don't think they do that in America. However, since we do not want to kill dozens of people at some such event, we would have to find some food that he likes but which the others do not. That may be difficult to do. Frankly, as I think more about it, I am having doubts about this whole approach. What if the president shows up but doesn't eat anything? What if he only takes a drink? What if he does nothing other than kiss his relatives and talk?"

As the excursion boat docked at the pier in Washington, Colonel Karam and Hassar went off to their rooms at the Zorita Hotel while Karasek went in search of Helena, hoping she performed her belly dances in the afternoon as well as in the evening. He often wondered whether he might persuade her to go to the Middle East with him after his 'business' in America was finished. He knew she would be a sensation. Unfortunately, she was so beautiful and so talented, some Sultan might just take her away from him.

17

The young woman reclined languorously on a small beige rug decorated with faded pink roses, some of whose petals disappeared in the cords of the frayed edges. All hope of indoor utility long since spent, the fragment of rug had been relegated to lining the bottom ribs of a canoe.

The young woman's back pressed against a large mauve pillow, also well-worn, covering a fan-shaped wooden backboard set upright near the bow. She was riding backwards, facing a young man seated at the rear who paddled in smooth strokes, alternating the paddle from side to side. The olive-skinned young man wore blue jeans, but was shirtless, thereby displaying a firm upper body, the muscles of which rippled as he paddled.

The young woman had done everything possible to create an aura of seduction. The hair of her blonde wig tumbled silkily down over her shoulders and feathered out across the bodice of a pale blue jump suit. Her knees were slightly raised above the bottom of the canoe, one knee a bit higher than the other—a position to her way of thinking infinitely more provocative than having her legs lying flat on the bottom. If her legs were splayed out flat, her thighs would certainly look fatter than they actually were. Being barefoot, she also made an effort to keep her toes pointed, thereby producing an attractive arch that ended in a row of carefully manicured, painted toenails. Her toenails were pale blue, matching her jump suit.

The young man did not seem to pay attention to any of this as he paddled. His gaze was fixed on the water and shoreline. Now the canoe was moving close to the Virginia shoreline of the Potomac River, gliding under overhanging tree branches. High cliff-like embankments, covered with trees that held budding green growth signifying early spring, rose skyward from the river. On both sides of the river, the high sheer walls muffled the sounds of the city, making the canoe seem to move in a deep secluded watery canyon. A fishing boat that had gone barreling by earlier, heading down river to Key Bridge, was the only sign of life that the couple had seen on their journey.

When the young woman looked to the side she could observe the canoe cutting through water so still it produced a nearly perfect reflection of the foliage overhead. Closer in, she was intrigued by the small ripple that angled back from the bow, distorting the watery image and making the reflected leaves appear to undulate in a frenetic dance.

She looked at the young man. She enjoyed staring at him, and as the occasional yellow rays of warm sunlight filtered down through the trees, flickering across his shoulders and chest, she drifted into a dreamy trance.

"Izzy," she asked softly, trying to catch his eye, "am I good in bed?"

After a lapse of a few seconds, he glanced at her. Then his eyes resumed their focus on a distant point ahead of the canoe. "How should I know, Marsha? We've never been in bed. I mean, not together." He continued staring straight ahead. "We've done it in the back seat of my car, against the dining room wall of your Aunt Sylvia and Uncle Saul's apartment, and on a chair in their kitchen."

So They Went and Elected a Jewish President

"Yes, I know. And I suppose that really isn't very romantic. I don't mind telling you that if we keep doing it against the dining room wall and on the kitchen chair, I'm going to need to find a good orthopedic surgeon." She turned to gaze over the side of the canoe, her head resting on an arm as she watched her fingers playing in the water. "Izzy, how come you never take me to your place? You've never even told me where you live. For all I know you could be living with a wife and five kids."

"That's not true. I have told you before. I live with several guys. I don't think it would look right for you to come over and shack up there. What would the guys think of you?"

"Who cares? I feel really loving toward you. They'd understand that."

"Well, I dunno."

"Then why don't you take me to a hotel? We could go to a hotel right after Oneg Shabbat and spend the rest of the weekend there. We could romp around naked for the whole weekend. We could loll around in a jacuzzi. Some of the better hotel rooms have jacuzzis, you know. We could have food sent in. It would be a blast."

"You mean, take a naked jacuzzi together?"

"Of course naked!"

"Well, I dunno."

"If you keep saying 'I dunno', you're going to make me angry. I know it isn't money. Heaven knows, you seem to have lots of money."

"Well, I dunno."

"There you go again. Isn't it up to the man to supply the place? I give of myself, but you, you're supposed to make the arrangements, and I hardly call jumping into the back seat of your car, making arrangements. But Izzy on another subject. You've met Harry Fishman, the president's father, at my place a few times."

"Yes. of course. We've talked together a lot. He always wants to know about Israel."

"Well anyway, Harry says he likes you but he wonders about you."

Izzy's eyebrows raised. "Why?"

"He says he's not sure you're one-hundred percent Jewish."

"What? I always thought either you're Jewish or you're not Jewish. How, for example, could you be eighty-five percent Jewish? Who could figure out that blood line?"

"He says you don't seem to be very familiar with Jewish expressions, you know, the lingo."

"What kind of Jewish expressions? Are you talking about Yiddish? To all of you New Yorkers, Yiddish is a second language. I come from Israel, we don't speak Yiddish there. OK, I have heard a little bit of Yiddish and I believe there's a Yiddish theater in Tel Aviv. But we speak Hebrew or we speak English." Izzy's tone had a touch of sarcasm as he said the word, English, because he often wondered if New Yorkers really spoke English.

"Harry also thinks you're too muscular to be Jewish. He says Jewish boys spend so much time studying Hebrew to prepare for their Bar Mitzvah and studying the bible, they haven't time to build muscles."

Izzy shook his head. "So to please you and Harry, I should stop working out four days a week at the gym and work out only two days?"

"Izzy, Izzy, take it easy. When Harry made the muscles comment, he had a big smile. It's an old joke."

But no matter what, Marsha found it impossible to break through Izzy's reserve. Marsha's mind was in a muddle. She really liked Izzy, but there seemed to be something he was holding back. Maybe he was afraid if they got too deep into the relationship she would press him to get married. And maybe he wasn't ready for that. There were times when she felt he really was in love with her, but then he would suddenly draw back. It was a puzzle, but then again, they hadn't been going together that long. Perhaps in a few months he would come around.

The afternoon was warm. Marsha opened a can of beer for Izzy and handed it to him. She opened one for herself. The first sip was cool and soothing.

Izzy had pulled the canoe into a tiny cove, and was now sitting on the rug-covered bottom of the canoe next to Marsha. "Marsha, tell me about your cousin, Arnold. You remember I met him at your aunt's apartment. He is thirteen, right? Isn't it time for his Bar Mitzvah?"

"Yes. It's coming up in June."

"What date? Maybe I can come."

"I think the first Sabbath in June. But the really fun part comes right after. The family is having a big party that night. They're pulling out all the stops. It'll be at the Washington Hilton. And best of all, it's going to be a Bar Mitzvah Costume Party!"

"Do you think the president will come?"

"We hope so. Arnold is his favorite. But considering his usually tight schedule, he might come either to the Bar Mitzvah itself, or to the party later. Probably not both and we don't know which one he'll come to. Why are you asking, does it matter?"

"Not really. I was just curious."

He leaned over to kiss her and as he did so he felt a drop of rain on the back of his neck. Her head was tilted back on the pillow as the next raindrop landed squarely in her eye. She lay there blinking the watery eye at him with a surprised look on her face. "It wasn't supposed to rain today."

"I know," Izzy said as he looked up at a huge black cloud that had come out of nowhere. All he had time to say was: "It's beginning to look pretty bad..." when the quiet surroundings erupted into a frenzy of white water. A sudden rush of wind swept down between the river's high walls. The sudden current coming down the river swept the canoe out of the cove and down the shoreline. When Izzy looked at the tree-lined shoreline it almost seemed as if the boat was stationary and the shoreline was rushing upstream. Soon, the river was swollen with the cloudburst, falling torrents of rain meeting up-shooting bursts of white foam.

Izzy scurried to the rear of the canoe, grabbed a paddle and forced the canoe farther out from shore. Partly at Marsha's urging, he decided to try crossing to the boathouse which lay downstream on the opposite side of the river. In the fury of the storm, the boathouse, safe and dry, was the only logical place they could think of to get to.

At first, Marsha tried to help with the paddling but her skills proved inadequate in the swift, choppy current. She almost turned them over before he shouted at her to stop and lie flat on the bottom of the boat.

Paddling frantically for the small pier at the boathouse next to Key Bridge, Izzy made it almost to midstream when he had to surrender to the combined fury of the wind, the torrential rain, and the tricky currents. He could no longer even see the bridge ahead of him.

Marsha lay huddled in several inches of water in the canoe bottom as Izzy came about and angled back towards the Virginia shoreline. A strange quirk in the currents seemed to make it easier to get to that side than the boathouse side.

As he maneuvered the boat in close to the shoreline, Izzy lunged for a low overhanging branch that was sweeping by. He managed to grab the slippery branch and then, holding on with all his might he began working in hand-over-hand pulling the boat to the embankment. He somehow managed to get one foot on shore, then he hopped out, one arm holding onto the branch, the other hauling the canoe onto a hollowed out area on the bank. Marsha crawled out of the canoe and slithered on all fours up the muddy bank, wet, bedraggled, and soon covered with mud. Her pale blue jump suit was torn on the knee and no longer pale or blue.

Several minutes later the two of them were huddled shivering under the overturned canoe.

He hugged her for awhile, and then, as she started to grow calmer, he tried to seduce her. He put his tongue in her ear. Her ear was filled with mud. "Ugh!" he said as he tried the other ear.

"That one is loaded with cotton," she said. "I have drops in it."

They struggled awhile in silence. She was aghast. He was trying to make love to her right there in the muck under the canoe with the rain beating a tattoo on the hull and the wind gusting around the sides. She pushed him partly away by the shoulders. "Izzy, what are you gonna do next? Really! First you're licking my ear, then you're slobbering all over my eye. Then you've got your tongue all over my neck. Next thing I know you'll be trying to get your tongue up my nostril or something!"

"But I love you, Marsha, and can't you realize, I want to kiss you all over."

"OK, why don't you *kiss* me then?" She held her face up with her lips in a tight pucker. "Here, kiss me. Now...wasn't that sweet? Izzy, I can see that you really don't like to kiss. All you want to do is lick, lick, lick. I want a boyfriend, not a dog."

At first, she resisted. She had never been so miserable in her life. But after awhile, she needed the warmth of his body, so she gave in.

An hour later, the rain let up and the river was calm enough for Izzy to attempt a return crossing. They made the journey in silence.

Later, in his car, Marsha looked over at him. "Izzy, tell me if I'm wrong, but I'm beginning to think that you don't want to make love unless we're on a hard kitchen chair, or up against some damned wall, or maybe under a wet freezing boat in a thunderstorm. Well, that's not my style. I need my creature comforts. No more sex, Mister, unless it's in a warm comfortable hotel room—and the more expensive the better."

But there was one thing Abu Aram, alias Izzy, could not do: romp naked around a hotel room with Marsha. Although he dearly wanted to romp around naked with Marsha, and although he really had fallen in love with her, he was now facing the biggest dilemma of his life.

* * * * *

Sylvia toyed with the eggs on her plate as Saul paced back and forth in their kitchen. "Saul, I have to tell you something you already know, but I'll tell you anyway. Our love life has gone to hell in a handbasket."

"Yes, I know."

"Is it due to work on those movies? You're putting in atrocious hours. And I can tell that the stress on you is terrible."

"Yes, I know."

"Well, what can you do about it?"

"I can't lower the stress or the workload but I may be able to see a doctor about it."

"What about that doctor you met at the embassy party? The Indonian Embassy, I think."

"He's in Indonia now."

"Doing what?"

"I dunno. Possibly he's collecting organs for his organ bank."

"Darling, I'm sorry it has come to this, but maybe you should make an appointment with him when he gets back."

* * * * *

Rose and Harry ordered an appetizer before the main course at the Four Seasons Restaurant in Georgetown. Harry looked glum.

"I take it this high life in Washington doesn't agree with you," Rose commented, as she reached over and speared a shrimp from Harry's plate.

"No, it doesn't."

"To tell you the truth, I too am getting a bit jaded by going to one party after another. And I've gained thirty pounds since David became president."

"I've gained twenty pounds."

"And I am really tired of people 'sucking up,' hoping I will talk to David about some dumb thing or other. We're not being invited because of who we are...not just Rose and Harry Fishman out of a little shop on Long Island. No. It's simply because of our son and if he doesn't get re-elected, as soon as he is out of office, the invitations will grind to a halt pretty quickly."

So They Went and Elected a Jewish President

"Rose, I feel the same way. In return for a few Swedish meatballs and roast beef sandwiches on the buffets, and a glass of wine, they all want a lot in return. And they almost can't believe that I can't and won't give them any information in return."

"My Secret Service 'spy' told me you slipped up to New York this past weekend while I was in Austin viewing some dumb movie produced by an independent studio. They had invited David, of course, but I showed up instead. So, why New York?"

"Yes, I did go up to Long Island," Harry admitted somewhat sheepishly. "I wanted to take a look at a very nice candy store with post office window inside and a pharmacy in the rear. It's pretty far out on the Island, at Islip. But it's in an area that is being developed, so I'm sure the business will grow. And the price was right."

* * * * *

Dr. Doctor gazed at the deep blue waters of the lagoon as he sat holding an exotic rum drink on the veranda of a large white residence. The Indonian Ambassador, newly returned home and since elected prime minister, sat just a few feet away.

"So, you were impressed with our Hupa Show in Washington."

"Yes, very much so."

"And I understand that you are a representative of the Organ Transplant Society of America. I also understand it is...aah...a bank of human sex organs...and you are here to discuss your program. Well, I have to tell you that our people, being well-endowed, have no need for further enhancement; however, our king is concerned that some of the male attendants to the queen are showing her too much attention. This is to be expected, of course, because she is the most beautiful woman in the islands."

"So, there is a possibility of your providing donations?"

"Yes."

"However, I must warn you that donations must be strictly voluntary. I don't want lawsuits later."

"This is not a problem," the newly elected prime minister said as he snapped his fingers and called for refills on the drinks. "Let me explain. Here in the Indonian Islands we have very high unemployment, especially among young men. We want to establish positions that you would refer to as 'eunuchs' to her majesty. These would offer a life of comfort and luxury that these men would otherwise never know. And since these men would be asexual, the king would be free to travel around the world without worrying if there was...aah...what do you call it? Yes, panky-hanky."

"Well, we actually call it 'hanky-panky,' but you are on the right track. When can we proceed?"

"You Americans are always in a hurry. Why don't we relax here in our beautiful setting while we have our drinks? Then, after dinner, you will be our guest at our local Hupa Show. It is much more spectacular than the one we were able to put on in Washington. And you will be able to examine firsthand a few of the eunuch candidates who will be appearing tonight."

"That sounds wonderful."

"I thought you'd say that. But first, let us talk money. You are certainly aware that a substantial sum of money will have to change hands before you can begin your collection operations. Furthermore, I have made inquiries into your organization and it does not appear to be well-financed."

"I am happy to say that the situation has changed dramatically. As you probably know, Oriental men are, in general, not well-endowed when it comes to the male organ. So, I went onto the Internet to advertise our services, focusing principally on the Orient. The response has been overwhelming."

"Fine. Then, how do you expect to pay?"

"I have, the doctor replied with a smile, "the money in my little black bag.

* * * * *

Roger Halstead sat at his desk in the West wing of the White House with his elbows propped on his desk and his face buried in his hands. He was mumbling to himself: "I can't believe it, but the president, despite two attempts on his life, still insists on riding his bike in downtown Washington every morning when he is not traveling. Now he wants to attend a Bar Mitzvah for his young cousin...Arnold, I think the kid's name is. Well, whether the president likes it or not, we will have security floating in the sky and hanging from the rafters."

18

It seemed to Izzy that the car came out of nowhere. One minute he was walking down the street after leaving Marsha off at her apartment; the next, he was being dragged into a car. The chloroform handkerchief put him into a tortured sleep. As the car drove through Washington, he had a dream that was both good and bad: the good was that he was having sex with Marsha; the bad that they were doing it in the woods in the middle of a bush covered with brambles.

The dream changed. Now he was being carried by Marsha. It occurred to him that she was stronger than he thought. She started pinching him all over. "Stop, Marsha," he mumbled as he twisted and turned on the bed.

"Who is Marsha?" Colonel Karam asked.

"His Jewish girlfriend," Karasek replied.

In the room at the Zorita Hotel, Izzy slowly came awake looking up into the eyes of General Karasek, Colonel Karam and the burly Hassar who were leaning over the bed, six hands pinching him to wake him up. That explains Marsha's pinching, Izzy thought.

"Abu, my young friend, you have been seeing much of the Jewish girl. Perhaps too much."

"You were the one who told me to get acquainted with her to infiltrate the family," Izzy said groggily. "That's exactly what I am doing, General. I am following orders."

"Perhaps too well."

"How can I follow orders too well?"

"Infiltrating does not mean becoming one of them."

"I have no intention of becoming one of them."

"Good. Now tell us, is the president coming soon to a family function?"

"I don't know."

"How could you not know if you have successfully infiltrated?"

"They don't tell me everything. Besides, no one knows whether the president will show up or not. They invite him all the time, but he never shows up."

"Did you not tell us before that the family has a thirteen-year-old boy. Does that not mean a Bar Mitzvah is coming up?"

"Yes, the boy, Arnold. And I can tell you that the family says Arnold is a favorite of the president."

"And when is the Bar Mitzvah?"

"The first Sabbath in June."

"And the details...?"

"I don't have any details."

"Will the president be there?"

"I don't know."

Unable to restrain himself, the burly Hassar who had been growing increasingly angry as he listened, reached down and lifted Izzy up. He held him in the air, his hands jammed under Izzy's armpits, and began a vigorous up and down shaking. In his weakened state from the chloroform, Izzy hung limply, unable to resist. His head lolled from one side to the other; his feet swung back and forth at crazy angles. Coins spilled from his pocket and splashed noisily onto the floor. The sections of the Hebrew Bible that he always carried, fell out of his back pocket onto the floor. Colonel Karam angrily kicked the taped-together chapters under the bed.

The shaking continued, becoming more and more vigorous.

"Stop," General Karasek commanded. "We do not want to shake him up too much!"

As Izzy was thrown down onto the bed, out of the corner of his eye he saw the two buckets. His eyes widened in sudden fear. He curled over on his side.

"Pull off his shoes and socks," Karasek commanded. "Then, put one foot in one bucket, the other in the other bucket."

Colonel Karam and Hassar roughly yanked off Izzy's shoes. They threw them noisily against the wall. They pulled off his socks. Hassar thought momentarily about keeping the socks. They were brightly colored argyles, but he changed his mind when he saw they were several sizes too small.

Yanking on his legs, they dragged the young man to the edge of the bed. They put one bare foot into the bucket of hot water; the other into the bucket of cold water.

"What happened to the ice?" Karasek asked angrily.

"We ordered it from room service hours ago, it must have melted while we were gone."

"He is not screaming," Karasek said in annoyance as he examined Izzy's foot in the bucket of hot water. "Why not?"

"Well, perhaps he is accustomed to being in hot water."

"Nonsense. There must be something wrong with the water. Aha! Tepid. Didn't you tell room service we wanted scalding water? What kind of an incompetent hotel have you two been staying at?"

Colonel Karam was apologetic. We can try to draw some hot water from the faucet in the tub."

Hassar, who rarely spoke, felt he had to say something. It was a complaint: "There is no hot water. I took a cold bath again this morning. Zumar, if we had stayed in a hotel run by my Libyan friends instead of your Iraqi friends, we would have plenty of scalding hot water and buckets of ice brought up whenever we wanted."

"Call room service," Karasek ordered Colonel Karam. "I know they cannot bring up a bucket of hot water if the hotel never has any hot water but at least they can bring up a bucket of ice."

"Ali, I'm sorry, the colonel said, "it is now five minutes past four and room service ends at four P.M. That is when the shift changes and they have not been able to hire anyone yet for the next shift."

Karasek shook his head. He slumped down in a chair in utter disgust. After slowly regaining his calm, he resumed questioning Izzy: "You have spoken of a Bar Mitzvah for the boy, Arnold. You know by my background, I am half-Jewish. I know something about these things, although I do not go to the synagogue."

Izzy, aware that the attempted water torture was a failure, laughed at Karasek in scorn. "How can you be half-Jewish? Either you're Jewish or you're not Jewish." But when Hassar made a menacing move towards him, Izzy decided to shut up.

"Beware, my young friend, because we have other methods of exacting information," the general warned. "Now tell me more about the family. I know that the Jewish faith in America has three levels: Orthodox, Conservative and Reformed. The family of the president belongs to which of these?"

Izzy, not being Jewish, wasn't sure. In Jerusalem he remembered seeing what he thought were Orthodox: black-clad men, some with wide-brimmed hats and some with fur hats, lined up at the Western Wall. However, he never remembered coming across Conservative or Reformed in Jerusalem. And although he was aware of the other levels in the United States, the line between Orthodox, Conservative and Reformed was not always clear to him. When he was in the synagogue with Marsha, he thought it was Conservative, but she said it was Orthodox. On top of that, he wasn't sure whether they went to an Orthodox synagogue because it was close or whether the whole family was, in fact, Orthodox. And maybe some were Orthodox and others Reformed. It was a puzzle to him. Nor did he want to take chances by asking too many questions. In answer to Karasek's question, he took what he thought would be a safe guess: "They're Orthodox," he said.

"That may well be," Karasek, who knew little or nothing about the Jewish religion in America, said in agreement. "I have watched as members of the family walked to the synagogue on the Sabbath, refusing to drive a car.

They do their grocery shopping on Friday's before sundown. Those are good indicators. And this is useful information."

But through it all, it was clear to General Karasek that the strain of waiting these long months was beginning to be evident among his cohorts. Colonel Karam and Hassar were becoming openly irritated with one another and there was one thing he knew: assassins had to pull together. There could be no animosity between them. He came to a decision. "We will let the young man go for now. We can always grab him off the street and chloroform him whenever we want. And as a special treat for you my friend, Zumar, and you Hassar, I am taking you out to dinner."

"Where?"

"The Purple Sphinx."

"Ali, are you trying to poison us?" Colonel Karam asked.

"Stay calm my friends. The Purple Sphinx is under new management. The food now is excellent and I have a special treat in store. There is music and a belly dancer who is a vision from the Arabian nights. For one night, you will dream that you are out of this accursed country. Helena will bring you, Zumar, to your homeland, to Baghdad; and you Hassar, to Benghazi, your home on the shores of the warm blue waters of the Gulf of Sidra.

"But remember, when the night is over, the young belly dancer leaves with me, and we leave alone. You two are free to go and find your own belly dancers."

*****

The car sped along the New Jersey Turnpike to New York. As General Karasek drove, he was annoyed at the way Colonel Karam fidgeted next to him on the front passenger seat. "Zumar, why can't you simply sit back and relax? Look at Hassar in the back seat. I believe he is asleep."

"He could sleep through an earthquake," the colonel replied.

"So much the better. What is there to do in an earthquake other than to remain calm and relaxed until the shaking stops?"

Colonel Karam closed his eyes and rested his head back against the headrest, but he did not sleep. "Ali," he asked, "why are we going to New York? What will we do there? Is this a holiday? Is this part of your plan to lighten our moods while we sit around waiting forever for another opportunity to kill Fishman?"

"I detect a complaint in your question. This trip is not a holiday. It is part of the plan. You may remember that Abu told us a Bar Mitzvah would take place in early June. It is for a favorite cousin, so the president may attend.

So They Went and Elected a Jewish President

If not, he may attend the party that night. We are going to Brooklyn to the home of the Lubavitch sect. You may have seen them on the American television. They represent the highest level of orthodoxy in America. Some consider them the holiest among the Jews. At Crown Heights in Brooklyn, I will arrange to purchase suitable garments for each of us: the black wide-brimmed hat and black suit. Fur hats are too hot for this time of year. When the time comes, we will of course, wear beards as well but we will either have to grow them or purchase them in a shop that sells such things to actors who perform on the stage."

"We are to be disguised as Jewish holy men? Ali, this is an abomination."

"We will attend the Bar Mitzvah at the synagogue. If the president shows up, it will be his last Bar Mitzvah. If he does not show up, we will also attend the party that night. Disguised as the holiest of Jewish men, no one would refuse to admit us."

"We are to attend a service in a synagogue? Allah would forbid this."

"Allah will not forbid this deception. You forget that we are doing this for Allah. We are carrying out the will of Allah."

"But why did you pick this Lubavitch sect? Who are they?"

"I am a fighting man; I confess I do not know much about religion. My religion is the sword, the dagger, the pistol. But if you recall, our young friend, Abu, said that Fishman's relatives are Orthodox. He said they were at the highest level of the three levels in America: Orthodox, Conservative and Reformed. Like Abu, I also remember seeing holy men in Jerusalem as they gathered to pray at the Western Wall. They were Orthodox I am sure. The garments can be purchased from one of the stores in Crown Heights."

"Why would they sell such garments to Arabs? And furthermore, Ali, how can you talk with Orthodox Jews? Do they speak English?"

"Again, Zumar, my friend, you forget that I am half-Jewish. When I am purchasing the garments, I will casually let my Israeli passport fall open on the counter. They will not refuse me. You underestimate me. I spent much time in Israel and I learned quite a bit of Hebrew."

"But what if they speak New York Jewish?"

"You mean Yiddish? Remember, my doubting friend, I have also spent a lot of time in New York visiting relatives. We bantered in English, Yenglish *and* Yiddish. And to complete the deception, I will be wearing a yarmulke. I picked up a nice one: it is silk-lined and covered with dark purple velvet embossed with a ring of simple white designs. As we enter the shop, you will each have a yarmulke to wear. I did not think you and Hassar wanted to spend the money, so yours are nothing fancy. I just bought plain black ones

127

for each of you. However, a warning: you and Hassar will keep your mouths closed while you are outfitted with the garments. It will be easy for Hassar because he does little more than grunt anyway. The way I see it, if you keep silent, the deception will be quite good because no one in the world can tell by looking at you that you are not Jewish."

"Ali, again, we blaspheme Allah."

"I think not. Remember it is written: Allah does not judge a man by the camel he rides, or by what he wears on his head to protect him from the desert sun, or by the folds of garment on his back. He judges by what is buried deep in a man's heart."

*****

Izzy sat in his car alone, brooding. After the episode in which General Karasek and his cohorts had tried the hot water for one foot and ice water for the other, Izzy had begun to feel a growing resentment towards these men. Although he had told the absolute truth to the conspirators: that no one knew whether the president would attend a particular function, they did not believe him. He was offended by this. He knew he could not trust these men. Further, he liked being in America. He had begun to feel at home here. What was there for him in Jerusalem anyway? He had no family. He would return to a turbulent state with no job, no resources. He did not want to spend his life throwing rocks at Israeli soldiers. There was more to life than that. There was Marsha. Whenever he gazed at her photograph in his wallet, he realized he was desperately in love with Marsha. Even if she had not had a forty-two inch bust, he knew he would still love her completely. He knew he had not been frank with her and it worried him that she might find out about his involvement with the conspirators. If that happened, it would be all over between himself and Marsha.

Then there was the matter of religion. In his comparative religion courses at the university, Izzy had become convinced that there really was only one God, and it seemed to matter not whether He was called Allah or Jehovah. These were simply the two faces of the one God. So, after much reflection, Izzy decided to take two of the most significant steps he had ever taken in his whole life: he would have himself circumcised and he would convert to the Jewish faith. Of course, until he healed, he knew there would be no sex with Marsha, but after that, it would not be covertly on a kitchen chair, or up against a wall in a dark dining room, no! It would be the whole nine yards, running around naked chasing Marsha in a hotel room, an expensive hotel room, the kind Marsha liked. In fact, why not a suite equipped with a king-sized bed, and a marble jacuzzi. They would drink pink champagne. He would ask her to marry him.

Izzy decided he would give no more information to the conspirators. He deeply regretted telling them that a costume ball was planned for the evening of Arnold's Bar Mitzvah, but the president was not likely to show up anyway, so maybe no harm done.

When he really thought about the whole business, he realized that he had been at best a fringe accomplice who never took an active role in the plot. He was privy to none of the details. It crossed his mind that he might tell some authorities that assassins were out to get the president, but what would he really be telling them that they did not already know? He could tell them that the assassins were staying at the Zorita Hotel in Washington, but he had no knowledge that they were still there. And if federal agents went to the hotel looking for spies and espionage agents, they would have had to arrest well over a hundred men since everyone at that hotel was either a spy or looked like a spy.

In any case, federal agents surely knew that someone is always out to get the president. On one hand, an assassin could be some kind of fanatic or on the other, an agent of a foreign government. Izzy knew that if he talked, he would be interrogated and locked up somewhere. So he said nothing.

Izzy also knew that he could never tell Marsha. This was a case where honesty was definitely not the best policy because he knew Marsha would never forgive him and never trust him again.

*****

Izzy sat in the doctor's office. The doctor was visibly confused.

"Why," he asked, "would a 21 year old young man, a Palestinian at that, want to be circumcised? When you got back home you would be ostracized by friends and family."

"I don't intend to go back to Jerusalem. I plan to live here in America."

"But still, even in America, you are an Arab."

"Not any more. I am taking a new name. I will become Isador Weinstein. I am converting to Judiasm."

"Is this a long held, heartfelt desire or is it because of a woman."

"It is because of a woman."

"She must be quite a woman to influence you to make such a basic change in your life."

"Doctor Levy, if you had such a woman, and let's say she was a catholic, I believe you would be seriously considering leaving Judiasm and converting to Roman Catholicism."

So They Went and Elected a Jewish President

19

It was the first Sabbath in June. In a voice thin and faltering at first, but later beginning to ring with confidence, young Arnold stood with the colorful silk Talis draped over his shoulders. He read the holy words from the Torah before a congregation of relatives and friends gathered for the occasion in the B'nai Sinai Synagogue in Silver Spring. Arnold's parents, Shirley and Hymie, had joined this synagogue shortly after moving down to Silver Spring from New York.

Arriving late for the service and leaving early, were three holy men who were thought to be from the Lubavitch sect. They had slipped into seats in the rear and spoke to no one. They attracted scant attention because all eyes were focused on Arnold, the Bar Mitzvah boy.

The president did not show up. Although he had planned to attend, a last minute crisis had developed. After noting his absence, hope became widespread that he might show up for the Bar Mitzvah celebration to be held that same night at the Washington Hilton Hotel. The affair would be at least as big as the Family Inauguration Blast with relatives and friends coming from far and wide. The affair was planned as a costume ball. A lavish and colorful event, it would be an American version of the Beaux Arts Ball in Paris.

*****

At the Oneg Shabbat in the social room following his Bar Mitzvah, Arnold proudly accepted the congratulations of the rabbi, the cantor, and well-wishers surrounding him. He basked in the warm glow of having attained manhood under Jewish law. But under the surface, something gnawed at him. He longed for the old days when Jewish law provided full entitlement. "Yes, today I am a man," he said to himself, "but they won't let me drive, go to R rated movies, go steady with a girl or have a couple of beers."

*****

On the evening of Arnold's Bar Mitzvah, as the guests arrived at the Washington Hilton Hotel, they entered through a small reception room that led to the party ballroom.

The receiving line was short, consisting of the proud parents, Shirley and Hymie Fishman, with young Arnold at their side. Shirley and Hymie were noticeably divergent in costume. Shirley was dressed as Betsy Ross with a

131

flowery bonnet, a floor-length gingham dress and a small American flag draped over one arm. Hymie, on the other hand, wore an olive branch encircling his head and a flowing white toga, portraying a senator of ancient Rome. Arnold had begged to be allowed to wear a gorilla costume but his parents insisted on his dressing as a Swiss mountain climber. He objected strenuously: "I hate being a mountain climber type. I couldn't even climb the rope in gym class at school."

"Arnold, darling," his mother said, "how would it look in front of the entire family to have an animal on stage making the Bar Mitzvah speech?"

Arnold's protestations got him nowhere, so he stood in the abbreviated reception line in a tyrolean hat with a colorful feather set at a jaunty angle and lederhose. A short coil of rope was wound around his left arm and in his left hand he held a silver-coated, cardboard, imitation ice ax. Arriving guests, uncertain about the ax, were happy when Arnold reached out to shake hands with the opposite hand.

Shirley had meticulously planned every detail of the affair including the food on the extensive buffet table. It was strictly kosher, and consisted of everything from chicken soup to nuts. The list of food items looked like it had been taken directly from the menu of a Jewish deli, and in fact, Shirley had contacted the deli caterer and told him to send abundant selections of everything on the menu.

Shirley had selected the champagne for the Bar Mitzvah toast and the musical selections to be played by the small band. She would later also designate the three gifts out of the many, many gifts which her son would ceremoniously open in front of the assembled guests.

Judging by the number of invitations sent out, the affair promised to be of mammoth proportions. Well over two hundred invitations had been sent out making it the largest family gathering since the family's Inaugural Blast. Many family members bemoaned one of the facts of life of modern families which over time became dispersed across the country: "It's a terrible shame; we never see one another; we only get together for briths, Bar Mitzvahs, Bas Mitzvahs, weddings, law school and medical school graduations and of course, funerals."

Although the principal reason for attending the function was obviously to honor the Bar Mitzvah boy, nevertheless an opportunity to shake hands with the president was a powerful additional motivator.

And so they came. The president's parents, Rose and Harry, came as historical figures, Rose as Marie Antoinette, Harry as an historically *inaccurate* warm and friendly, smiling Napoleon Bonaparte. Harry remembered that Napoleon always had one hand slipped inside the front of his jacket, but he couldn't remember which hand. "What do you think, Rose? Which hand?"

"What difference does it make? Don't make such a big deal out of it. Just stick one hand in and when the other hand gets tired of shaking hands, just switch hands. Napoleon is dead; he could care less."

Sylvia and Saul Steinberg swept in next. Sylvia looked lovely as a southern belle in a shimmering pink hoop skirt covering six petticoats. Saul, with a newly grown small mustache and white suit, looked dashing as her escort. The costumes had been borrowed from Saul's movie set.

Inside at the bar, Harry approached Saul while their wives drifted away to see friends. "Saul, are those costumes from your movie set?"

"Yes. Just an overnight loan."

"Correct me if I'm wrong but aren't you dressed as Rhett Butler and Sylvia as Scarlett O'Hara?"

"Yes, that's right."

"I take it that the actor you tried to get to play Rhett Butler didn't pan out and you're playing the part."

"Right again."

"But you told me Sylvia would not play Scarlett because of the nude scene. Why did you change your mind?"

"I didn't. We still have nurse Sandra in the part. Sylvia is only wearing the gown for tonight."

"Forgive me for prying into your business but I'm curious. Did you ever find another General Robert E. Lee?"

"An hour after that other guy left, there were half-a-dozen waiting in line. In fact, the guy we picked had actually been in the army. He knew all about horses because he had been in the Old Guard at Fort Myer. I tell you, Harry, when that guy whistled, those horses swam across the river like they were in the Kentucky Derby"

"So how are the movies coming?"

"Right now, we're about fifty percent of the way through the first picture, the new, *Gone With The Wind,* and about thirty percent of the way through the second one. Can't tell you the title of the second one because I haven't thought it up yet."

"But while you're working don't you need some kind of title? How do the actors know what they're supposed to be doing?"

"You're right, of course. We have what we call a 'working title'. We call it Movie No. 2."

"My, how imaginative," Harry commented as he left Saul and walked across the room to mingle with the other guests.

*****

Meanwhile, the receiving line was in full swing as guests popped one-by-one from the line into the party room. The wide diversity of dress coming off the line gave the impression of a garment factory plagued with schizophrenic management.

In the line in the ante room, Rachel and Herman were kissing Arnold and patting him on his Tyrolean head. Rachel's matronly figure lent itself well to her depiction as Queen Elizabeth the First. Herman, who had served a short stint in the Navy, came as the famous Admiral Lord Nelson, complete with three-cornered hat and gilt-handled, gold tasseled fake sword.

But one young lady attracted all the attention, at least from the men. It was Marsha, dressed in a green sequined, shimmering, almost but not quite, see-through gown as the seductive Queen of Egypt, Cleopatra. History records that Cleopatra was not the beauty depicted by Hollywood. The real Cleopatra was apparently rather plain looking, and without much in the way of physical embellishments. Maybe, if Cleopatra hadn't been ruler over all of Egypt with a fortune in gold at her feet, no one would have paid any attention to her. It might be that Caesar and Marc Antony were only after her money and power. But Marsha's radiant beauty had young men salivating even though she did not have more than a couple of dollars in her green silk purse and three at-the-limit credit cards.

Following close behind Marsha was a young man whose dark complexion, turban and Egyptian robes made him look for all the world like Marsha's Nubian slave. And judging by the hold Marsha had on Izzy's affections, no statement could have been closer to the truth.

While greeting the line of guests one-by-one, Arnold looked up startled to see three black-clad rabbis with broad-brimmed black hats, standing next in line. Hymie whispered to his son that they were Hassidic holy men. And, in fact, as the first man approached, he leaned over Arnold like a huge black shadow, saying: "Sholom. Mazel tov!" Grabbing Arnold's earlobe, he gave it a firm but friendly tug.

"See," Hymie whispered in Arnold's ear, "didn't I tell you who they were? Your old man knows about these things."

The second holy man, however, said something that sounded like: "Shelem. Mexel tev." He was about to grab Arnold's earlobe when Arnold threatened him with the ice ax.

The third man said nothing at all. All he did as he shook hands was let out a soft, polite grunt.

So They Went and Elected a Jewish President

As the three holy men proceeded into the ballroom, Arnold was puzzled: "Dad, I heard the second man say, 'Shelem. Mexel tev.' What the hell is that?"

"Son, first of all, don't use curse words. It is not fitting on such a day. The poor man probably has a bad head cold which made his words sound funny."

"But the third man said nothing at all."

"Yes, and he is probably the holiest of all. I'm sure he has taken a vow of silence. When you're older, Arnold, you'll understand that your father knows about such things."

*****

And so the guests munched, drank, mingled, talked, laughed and danced. The ladies fluttered around Arnold telling him how honored and thrilled he should be that his cousin, the president of the United States, was coming to his party. With a lackadaisical shrug and a distinguishable note of sarcasm, Arnold replied, "I'll believe he's coming when I see the large whites of his eyeballs."

Shirley, standing directly behind her son, quietly screwed a knuckle deep into his buttock, momentarily making the boy's own eyeballs bulge out large and white.

Finally, the time came for Arnold's speech. His mother called him aside before he went up to the stage. "Arnold, I want you to leave the ice ax at our table. We don't want the guests to feel threatened. And remember, stand up straight and give a nice talk."

With that, Shirley propelled her son to the bandstand where he tripped and became momentarily entangled in the mountain climbing rope. Happily, Rabbi Mordecai was on the bandstand waiting for Arnold. It took every bit of skill that the rabbi possessed to unwind the rope. Finally, Arnold was able to throw the coil of rope on the floor like the biblical Adam rejecting the serpent.

After a brief fanfare from the band, the audience hushed. Rabbi Mordecai was brief. He congratulated Arnold and then turned the microphone over to the Bar Mitzvah boy. Gathering his composure, Arnold began: "Today I am a man and for this I owe the deepest gratitude and thanksgiving to my dear mother and father, to the wonderful teachings of Rabbi Mordecai who was kind enough to come down from New York for this occasion and to my other teachers..."

Arnold's voice rang out with a growing timbre of confidence because he knew it was a good speech. When his friend, Simon Golden, had given the speech at his own Bar Mitzvah several months before, Simon said there

135

wasn't a dry eye in the audience. It was so good Simon asked ten dollars for a copy of it. When Arnold read it over however, he came to the conclusion that it was too flowery for his taste and he would have to cut out about twenty percent. So eight dollars was all he would pay and just about all he could afford. But Simon refused to discount the speech. He said it was already discounted because he had paid fifteen dollars to Tisha Goldman who got it off the Internet. "Well I can get it off the Internet too," Arnold had told Simon. But it proved to be an empty threat because Simon told him that Tisha had worked for days before he found it, and although Arnold was pretty good on the Net, he wasn't good enough to find a speech like this. So, reluctantly, Arnold ponied up the ten dollars and then committed the speech to memory.

The ten dollars was well spent because only about a third of the way through the speech, as Simon had said, there wasn't a dry eye in the place. Several women sobbed openly. Even a few of the waiters had tears glistening in their eyes. But Arnold was destined not to finish. The band suddenly began playing again. He turned around confused. Did they think the speech was over? How could they? But as the strains of *Hail to the Chief* rang out, Arnold realized what was happening. The president was arriving. The audience rose to its feet and began applauding.

Indeed, the president was coming through the door but there was a problem: six men entered the room in a group: three Abraham Lincolns complete with beards and stovepipe hats, accompanied by Spiderman and two other famous masked heroes, Zorro and Batman.

The holy men who were seated in a huddle at a table in the corner, deep in conversation, straightened up, then stood up. General Karasek instantly detected the trick. It was the same as with the helicopters. Several helicopters flying together so no one would know which one carried the president. Tonight, in the arriving party, the same deception: the three Lincolns were virtually identical. Even his relatives couldn't tell which Abraham Lincoln was the president. It was obvious that none of the others, Spiderman, Zorro, or Batman could be the president because they were too short. Also they were walking backwards, keeping an eye on the crowd as befitted the Secret Service.

As soon as the entourage entered, the doors to the party room were closed.

All eyes were on the newcomers as the three Abraham Lincolns stepped up onto the bandstand. Two fell back as one stepped forward to put his arm around Arnold. He jokingly put his stovepipe hat on Arnold's head. The hat almost covered Arnold down to the shoulders. He tilted it back so he could peer out under the brim. The audience was still standing and applauding. Speaking into the microphone as the audience hushed, David Fishman said: "Sholom! I want to congratulate Arnold on his Bar Mitzvah and tell all of you how happy I am to be here tonight. And Arnold, I'm sorry I missed the first part of your speech."

Cries rang out from the audience for Arnold to do it over. "Arnold, take it from the top again. Take it from the top," rang out from all parts of the audience.

David Fishman smilingly took the stovepipe hat off Arnold's head and, stepping off the bandstand, took a seat at a place reserved for him. The large table next to the dance floor was now occupied by a colorful collection of historical and fictional characters. First, there was the American president sitting between his parents. To a casual observer, one would wonder about seeing Abraham Lincoln with his arms around Marie Antoinette and Napoleon. Also seated at the table were Arnold's parents, Betsy Ross and a Roman senator. And sandwiched in with the group were Spiderman, Zorro, and Batman.

Arnold began again. As he did it occurred to him that if Simon Golden knew he was giving the speech twice that night, he would have charged twenty dollars.

The applause at the end was thunderous. Once again, David Fishman stepped up onto the bandstand and embraced his young cousin. Turning to the audience he said: "I'm sorry my wife, Lisa could not be here tonight to enjoy this festive occasion, but she sends her love to one and all."

Rachel poked her husband Herman in the ribs. Seeing that, one would be left to wonder if Queen Elizabeth ever poked Lord Nelson in the ribs. "You'll notice," Rachel whispered, "David didn't give a reason why Lisa didn't come. He just said he was sorry she didn't come. That's one thing I always liked about David, no baloney about her being in bed with a cold, or tied up with some important group. He has integrity. He wouldn't lie for anyone, not even his spouse, unlike some of the past presidents we've had."

"But Rachel," Herman whispered back, "he said she sends her love to one and all. Now you know that's a damn lie."

"Not necessarily. She probably did say it although we all know she didn't mean it."

*****

The merriment went on for hours. The president finally broke away from the men who kept throwing questions to him about the economy, defense, Medicare, health care, you name it...

He walked over to his mother, Rose, and asked her to dance; then he danced with Arnold's mother, Shirley; then Sylvia and finally Rachel. As he danced with Rachel, he whispered in her ear: "I understand you're interested in serving the government."

"Yes, Mr. President, but I know your stand against nepotism."

"Rachel, it's only nepotism when the individual isn't fully qualified for the job. I have a job in mind that you are well qualified for. It's a diplomatic post. How would you like to be an ambassador? Just a small country for openers. Of course, you'd have to relocate for a few years and maybe Herman wouldn't want to leave his construction business on the Island, but if you're interested, call my Chief of Staff, Roger Halstead, on Monday morning."

After the dance, Rachel almost staggered back to her seat. She sat down next to Herman and stared at the wine glass on the table in front of her. "Rachel, what's the matter? Are you feeling well? You look white as a sheet."

"Herman, could my brother, Hymie, run your construction business for a couple of years?"

"I suppose so. He needs a job. I guess I could train him. But why do you ask? What's this all about?"

"My dear, you are looking at Rachel Fishman Schlotsberg, ambassador to... someplace. I don't actually know where yet."

"David has made you an offer?"

"That's right. While we were dancing. Everyone knows that Shirley Temple who was born singing and dancing, became an ambassador. Herman, do you think that David was not only influenced by my diplomatic potential but also because of my dancing?"

"I doubt it. With all due respects, you never could hold a tune, and although you're a good dancer, you never could tap dance like Shirley Temple!"

*****

As Arnold went over to open one of the gifts, the bomb went off. It was not a powerful bomb because it was intended only as a diversion. But it was loud enough to cause screams, cries and general tumult. Several of the gifts were destroyed in a cloud of black smoke.

At the sound of the blast, the holy men rushed forward and crowded around the three Abraham Lincolns trying to stab whichever Lincoln was president. The Lincolns looked so much alike that although the assassins kept watching during the evening to keep an eye on which one was actually the president, they felt they were caught in a pea and shell game. In the confusion, the assassins tried to stab all three. One Lincoln received a cut on the leg, another a stab wound on the shoulder. The third managed to escape Hassar's dagger by spilling hot coffee on him. After the lightning swift attack, the three assassins were out the door and rushing through the ante room to the hall outside. In hot pursuit of the assassins were Spiderman, Zorro, and Batman.

The assassins elbowed their way through a huge crowd that had gathered when word went out that the president was inside attending a party.

General Karasek separated from his compatriots and jumped into an open elevator. As he rode up, he hurriedly slipped off the black suitcoat jacket and turned it inside out converting it into a light blue sports jacket. He rode up two floors, then, holding the elevator doors open, he jammed the black hat, false beard, rubber gloves and dagger into the crack between the door and the inside wall where the items fell into the greasy muck at the bottom of the elevator shaft. Then, after pushing the button for every floor on the control panel, he stepped out of the elevator and went to his room.

After elbowing their way through the crowd, Colonel Karam and Hassar ran into a nearby men's room. They rammed their daggers down to the bottom of a wall-mounted trash receptacle. Inside the toilet stalls, each man slipped off his black jacket and turned it inside out converting the jacket into a well-tailored gray pinstripe suitcoat. Each jacket had an emblem signifying the Syrian Embassy embroidered on the breast. Stripping off the beards and rubber gloves they flushed them down the toilets. Next came the broad-brimmed black hats. The crowns had been attached to the wide brims with velcro fasteners. When the velcro was undone, the crowns were turned inside out converting them to dark blue pocket handkerchiefs. The brims, when separated and split open became cummerbunds which they tied around their waists with attached ribbons that fastened in the back.

Leaving the men's room, Colonel Karam and Hassar mingled with the chaotic milling throng outside the party room.

The rumor mill was in full swing. Rumors ranged from "...the president has been assassinated..." to "...the president has been stabbed but is alive..." to "...the president stabbed three assassins..." to "...President Abraham Lincoln has been assassinated...*again*..."

The simple fact was that the president escaped injury, and two Secret Service men who, like the president, also posed as Abraham Lincolns, received minor wounds. They were being treated in the party room by a medical crew that always followed the president just in case he or a member of his entourage required medical attention.

After the president was ushered out through a side door, the remainder of the guests were detained for questioning.

Arnold stood near the black-scarred table looking at the remains of several mangled gifts. He noted happily, however, that the envelopes containing the money gifts were located on a small adjacent table and had escaped the blast. Relatives who noted that their gifts were among those that had been damaged or destroyed assured Arnold that replacements would come very soon by UPS.

Outside in the hall, Colonel Karam and Hassar found themselves surrounded by Secret Service agents. Despite their protestations that they were diplomats attached to the Syrian Embassy, they were taken into custody.

Colonel Karam did not go quietly. "I see you American police are still making arrests based on racial and ethnic profiling. I thought that abominable and discriminatory practice had been stopped in this country."

*****

Izzy was astonished when he came up on the elevator to the party room floor. Earlier, he had become so upset that Marsha was dancing with every young man at the party, he never could get close to her. In a fit of jealousy he had left the party early and gone outside of the hotel where he spent an hour walking around the block. Tired of the walking, he had gone into the hotel bar where he ordered a stiff double martini. Returning to the floor of the party room after the assassination attempt, he put on his yarmulke and was let back inside where he walked over to Marsha.

Marsha was upset. "Izzy, where the devil were you? Do you realize some men tried to assassinate the president? Look at the smoke and Arnold's damaged gifts. But thank heaven they failed. Again, where were you?"

"Marsha, let me be frank. I was very upset that you were paying attention to every guy in this place except me. If I don't mean that much to you then we might as well end it right now."

"I admit that I got carried away by it all, but I really do love you, darling. If you can snap out of that mood you've been in lately. Moody men drive me bananas."

"Do you really love me?"

"Of course. Do I have to hit you over the head? How come we haven't done...you know...in a long time? I was beginning to think you really didn't love me."

"But Marsha, I do. Tell you what. Let me book a room in the hotel for tonight. A fancy hotel like this must have one with a jacuzzi. We'll run around naked like you always wanted."

So They Went and Elected a Jewish President

"Well, now you're getting somewhere, Izzy. Like I always said, I have to have my creature comforts."

*****

Colonel Karam and Hassar were being held in custody, but the third man in the plot was nowhere to be found.

A short time after the assassination attempt, government agents unlocked the door to Karasek's room and rushed in. They found him seated at a small table in his bathrobe, reading a newspaper and sipping a cognac. His bed was rumpled as if it had just been slept in. His sport jacket hung innocently on a hook near the door.

"I have just arisen from a nap. What is the problem, gentlemen?" Karasek asked coolly. "Are you in the habit of breaking into hotel rooms? Is this a robbery?"

Surrounded by agents, Karasek calmly leaned back in the chair. They demanded an I.D.

Karasek pulled out his Israeli passport and other papers indicating that he was an international salesman, currently in Washington to discuss sales of religious articles made in Israel. "Many Americans crave objects such as models of the Bethlehem manger with the baby Jesus surrounded by loving animals. We also have delicately carved statues of the Three Wise Men, crucifixes, models of the Church of the Holy Sepulcher. And these are authentic, having been produced in the land where all this took place. And, we are not limited to crafts. No, we have paintings of the Holy Family, and many watercolors, including those of Mary's Well in Nazareth. And for Jewish people who see Israel from a different standpoint, we have models of the tomb of Abraham, models of Mount Masada and the Western Wall. Turning to linens, we have..."

Shaking his head, the agent in charge said: "This couldn't be one of them. Let's get out of here before he winds up selling us some of this stuff."

After hearing the agents acknowledge that he was not the one they were looking for, Karasek demanded that they show him *their* I.D.s, which he then carefully inspected, holding up each picture badge to match it with its owner's face. He then chastised them with a brief lecture to knock before you enter a hotel room.

The government agents backed out of the room uttering deep apologies. As they hurried down the hallway to the next room, Karasek shouted after them: "Kindly remember to knock before you enter another room!"

*****

After four hours of intense interrogation, Colonel Karam and Hassar were released. Although the federal agents were highly suspicious of the pair, they had no hard evidence that they were the culprits. And, no matter what, the suspects were protected by diplomatic immunity. The State Department would of course, find some justification for having the suspects expelled from the country.

On the way back to the Zorita Hotel, Colonel Karam was not happy. They had failed in their mission. But Hassar, on the other hand, who never quite understood the full implications of the success or failure of any mission he had been involved in, was smiling and grunting happily.

"Why the happy grunts, you idiot?"

"It is quite simple," Hassar replied. "As the Americans say, 'With three strikes we are out...out of here.' Soon I will be lying on the warm sand on the beach at Benghazi with my sweetheart, watching the full yellow moon rise over the Gulf of Sidra. I will remove her veil and we will kiss. And perhaps, after being turned down by her for marriage for the second time, she will now agree to become my bride. You see, my fond hopes always remain alive."

Colonel Karam raised his eyebrows in surprise. "This is the first time," he said to himself, "that I have heard this oaf utter a complete sentence, and I hope he does get married and has a big family so I do not have to work with him again."

*****

Twenty-four hours after the assassination attempt, Roger Halstead paced the floor in his office in the White House as he berated the chief of the Secret Service who was seated head down, staring at the tracks Halstead had made in the carpet. It seemed to the chief that there must have been many such confrontations to produce an almost threadbare path in the expensive wool. Even part of the eagle's head was gone.

"How, Halstead demanded, "could three assassins pass undetected through your metal detectors with knives hidden on them?"

"They didn't get knives through the detectors."

"Well, where in hell did they get them?"

"Simple," answered the chief. "There were, as you may recall, three carving stations and after everyone had been served, the carvers left their stations trying to get a dance with that young lady...the cousin of the president...the one with the miniskirt and the big _____."

EPILOGUE

The president's parents, Rose and Harry Fishman, returned to Long Island at the end of their son's first term in office, where they opened a new candy store. As in the past, they lived in an apartment over the store. Rose, weary of the Washington social scene, returned happily to banging the broomstick on the floor over the store to let Harry know when it was time to come up for lunch. Since he was better financed than previously, Harry was able to turn more and more of the operation over to hired help. But, as usual with hired help, they always knew they could relax and goof off whenever they heard the broomstick bang because they knew the boss would disappear upstairs for a meal and a nap.

Harry, who had never managed to fit into the Washington social scene, was delighted to be back on the Island surrounded by old friends in the steam room. The insider stories he told about the things that went on in Washington were enough to make his damp-towel-covered friends shake their heads in disbelief. And when strangers who learned he was the president's father asked if he had another son who might run for president after David was out of office, Harry was quick to reply: "No! I had only one son to give for my country. And one is enough!"

*****

Saul Steinberg completed his remake of *Gone With The Wind.* The picture received only one-and-a-half stars from the critics. The movie was also not well-received by audiences mainly because Dr. Doctor's voluptuous nurse, Sandra, who had been recruited to play Scarlett O'Hara, walked off the set halfway through shooting and married one of the doctor's organ transplant patients. The pair were said to be on a perpetual honeymoon somewhere in the South. Saul knew his movie was severely hampered and perhaps terminally damaged by Sandra's departure. He had hoped that when it was finished, he might salvage two-and-a-half stars, but one-and-a-half stars was a crushing blow. After Sandra's departure, the men in the audience found it boring sitting through the second half of the movie. The burning of Atlanta, the South's defeat, and the final scenes between Rhett and Scarlett went over poorly. The discomfiture became almost painful when these scenes showed no more than distant shots using a stand-in for Sandra or indoor shots in which Scarlett's voice was supposedly heard through a closed door.

Saul's second movie, which he titled *Native American Revenge,* was considerably more successful. He reluctantly gave up the idea of making two side-by-side movies of the Civil War because the editing was so confusing even he couldn't always tell which picture he was working on. It was Harry Fishman, the president's father, who guided Saul in a different direction. He said American audiences always loved a good Indian movie. Thus inspired, Saul scripted a picture that told the story of an attack on the City of Washington in the late 1800s by a coalition of Native American tribes. At the climax, Senecas, Shoshones, Mohicans, Cherokees, Blackfeet, Seminoles, Navajo, Apache, Sioux, Choctaw and Chippewa massed on the upper reaches of the Potomac River several miles northwest of the city. In councils of war, the Indian chiefs were vocal: "In 1776, the first American Revolution was the white man's rebellion against the great white king across the sea. This is 1876, the Native American Revolution. We will send the white man back to live with the great white king across the sea."

The movie received three stars. Audiences especially liked the scene where the Indians circled the White House on horseback demanding the president's scalp. In the end, however, the Indians were forced back to their reservations. Their revenge eventually came in the form of establishing gambling casinos on the reservations which emptied the pockets of the white men who came to play their roulette tables and slot machines. The white men did not lose their scalps, they lost their shirts.

Although Saul had long protested that there was nothing wrong with him 'down there,' he eventually became so concerned, he finally agreed to receive an implant from the S.O.B. Division of OTSA. After the operation, Saul's wife, Sylvia, was delighted with his newfound sexual prowess. She could hardly wait for his visits to the trailer during breaks in the filming. And so, Dr. Doctor's most famous patient, a relative of the president, made the Sex Organ Bank of the OTSA a household name across America. In fact, whenever Saul appeared in the shower room at his health club, after glancing at his enhanced genitalia, the members would break out in spontaneous applause. Saul was at first puzzled by this until he remembered reading something about ancient Rome in the time of the Caesars. In those days, men and women bathed naked together in Rome's famous baths. Upon the appearance of a curvaceous woman or a well-endowed man, the huge crowds would show their approval in a round of applause.

Sylvia went on to give birth to a beautiful baby girl. One day, when the child was a year old, Saul asked: "Sylvia, I love baby Rebecca dearly; she is such a sweet child, but do you think she's Jewish?"

"Why do you ask that? She's our child, isn't she?"

"Of course, she's our child, but the red hair and green eyes..."

"I have wondered about that myself," Sylvia replied. I don't recall there having been any red hair and green eyes in either of our families, but the other day when I gave her a cup of chicken matzoball soup that I forgot to put the matzoball in, she cried out, "Oy gevalt!"

"She must be Jewish!" both agreed.

*****

Rachel Schlotsberg was appointed ambassador to the Indonian Islands located in the Banda Sea in a remote corner of the South Pacific. Her husband, Herman, accompanied her to the islands. On their arrival, the people gathered around Rachel and asked if she could sing and tap dance like Shirley Temple.

Rachel really loved the islands, and she did not really mind the way the dawns came up with Mandalayan thunder, but the startling flashes of silver lightning on a crimson horizon scared her as she lay in bed with the covers pulled up over her head. She also abhored the nakedness of the Hupa dancers. Herman, on the other hand, never tired of watching the female dancers throw curves that would have made a major league pitcher green with envy.

But one topic of discussion was absolutely forbidden. It was a serious crime under Indonian law to openly question why cages filled with monkeys were shipped into the large white building that stood in the center of the capital city, and why cases of soup were trucked out of the same building directly to the ocean terminal for export.

*****

Shirley and Hymie Fishman returned to Long Island where Hymie took over temporary management of Herman's construction business while the Schlotsbergs were living in the Indonian Islands. Hymie embarked on a major construction project, building many hundreds of townhouses on Long Island. The development was complete with beautiful indoor malls and a beach surrounding a placid lake. At the intersection of Shirley Avenue and Hymie Boulevard people could rent canoes and rowboats for an outing on Fishman Lake. Nor was Herman completely overlooked in the naming process, because when completed, Long Island's famous Levittown was completely eclipsed by Schlotsbergtown.

*****

Marsha and Izzy were married soon after Arnold's Bar Mitzvah. Izzy's moods had completely disappeared now that the assassins were no longer in the U.S., and also because he was now a bona fide member of the Jewish faith, with a completely healed circumcision. He was now free to run around their apartment naked chasing Marsha. Because Marsha had previously questioned Izzy's Jewishness, he always ran wearing his yarmulke.

Not long after their marriage, Marsha and Izzy had decided to settle down in a Washington suburb where Marsha gave birth to twin boys. One day when the boys were toddlers, Marsha was wheeling them in a double carriage when a woman passing by inquired about them, saying they really looked intelligent. Marsha replied proudly: "The one on the left is a doctor; the one on the right is a lawyer."

Whenever she was able, Marsha assisted her husband in running their deli. Although Izzy had acquired a taste for Jewish food, difficulties arose whenever he tried to add some Arabian delicacies to the display cases. "These were the foods of my youth," he proclaimed. But Marsha was quick to respond: "No, no, dammit, NO! Jewish food attracts Israelis. Arab food will attract Palestinians. We want peace. We do not want to have Middle East fighting right here in our little deli."

*****

When young Arnold came of age, he decided against a career in politics because he was dismayed at the numerous attempts made on his cousin, David's life. He enrolled in medical school, fulfilling a preordained destiny formulated for him while he was still a tiny fetus in his mother's womb.

*****

Just about all of the other relatives of David Fishman including second cousins, third cousins, long lost cousins, friends of cousins and coworkers of cousins had long since returned to their former homes by the end of his first year in office. One by one, they had become completely fed up with the red tape needed to land a government job, the high cost of living in Washington, the abominable traffic backups, and in most cases, the lack of a single damned invitation to an embassy party or a dinner at the White House.

*****

General Ali Moishe Karasek made a brief visit to the Middle East, where he was reprimanded by no less than five governments for failing to assassinate the U.S. president. He, of course, laid all the blame on Colonel Karam and Hassar, arguing that successful espionage was strongly dependent on teamwork and with two weak members of a three-man team, what did these officials expect? "I could have done better alone," he said in protest.

Having spent the counterfeit American money, the general had no choice but to begin using genuine money from his numbered Swiss bank account as he vacationed in Cannes, Nice and Monte Carlo. He and the former belly dancer, Helena, from the Navel Jewel in Georgetown, who now went by her real name, Mary Shaughnessy, strolled hand-in-hand among the movie stars during the Cannes Film Festival. Bystanders were convinced she was a famous movie star although no one could quite think of her name. They were convinced beyond doubt that Karasek in a well-tailored, immaculate white suit and flowery tie was the head of some big Hollywood studio. Although no one could think of his name or the name of the studio.

To Mary Shaughnessy's credit, she was completely unaware that Karasek had made three attempts on the life of the American president. While on the French Riviera, Karasek refused to let Mary apply for belly dancing jobs in any of the casinos. He insisted that she dance only for him on the balcony of their suite overlooking the blue Mediterranean.

When Karasek left for an assignment in Central America, Mary moved to Boston where she enrolled as an MBA candidate at Boston University. Her tuition and expenses were covered by her earnings as a parttime belly dancer at student smokers in fraternity houses. Additional earnings came from courses she taught at Boston's famous Belly Dance Academy.

General Karasek was last seen in Managua, Nicaragua. He had an ideal assignment because it involved one of the things he loved best: the opportunity to assassinate the leader of a country. However, several days after he arrived, he learned that it would be four-to-six weeks before he could begin serious preparations because the doctor said it would take that long for his system to recover from Montezuma's Revenge.

*****

After two rejections, Hassar finally married his longtime sweetheart, Rana, in a colorful ceremony in Benghazi. They said their vows on the beach overlooking the sparkling Gulf of Sidra. When their first boy was almost two years old, Rana was dismayed as she slowly came to the conclusion that her baby, solid, square, heavy-jawed, with the build of a gorilla, would probably grow up to be a carbon copy of his father. And she became sure of it when her efforts to get the baby to utter his first words resulted only in a series of grunts. "Soon I'll have to put up with two people grunting around the house all day," she moaned.

*****

Colonel Zumar Karam fidgeted on a chair as he waited for an interview with a high Iraqi official in the bombed-out shell of an office building in Baghdad. The official, not really anti-American, but decidedly anti-Jewish, was not pleased. In fact, he was seething. He demanded an explanation for the three failures. The colonel squirmed as he blamed the mess on General Karasek. "He was the leader. The responsibility for the failures lies squarely on his head. And with all due respect, I never quite understood how the planners of this mission ever thought a man who was part Jewish would assassinate a Jewish president."

Despite his claims of innocence, the colonel was reduced two steps in rank to major. He was assigned to monotonous guard duty at a warehouse in Baghdad. He could usually be seen fidgeting on a bench outside of the warehouse front door, cleaning his fingernails with the pointed end of a menacing-looking dagger.

The espionage community never heard of him again.

*****

After a successful four-year term in office, David Fishman went on to be re-elected in a vote which the Democrats called a landslide, but one which Republicans referred to as a mudslide. Fishman's accomplishments in office were many including the complete elimination of the national debt which freed up billions in former interest payments for use in ensuring that every American child could get a heavily subsidized college education. In the field of health, Americans received substantial federal aid for medical care and prescription drugs.

Average life expectancy rose 6.7 years as a result of the administration's aggressive health care program and environmental cleanup efforts. Joblessness was virtually eliminated due to the robust economy with inflation running less than one-and-a-half percent.

In international affairs, despite continuing diplomatic efforts by Fishman and his top policymakers, the Middle East was still caught up in its never-ending turmoil. There were frequent border clashes between Israel and its neighbors, Lebanon and Syria. Eruptions between the Palestinians and Israelis filled daily newspapers and TV newscasts. The single significant accomplishment came in regard to the holy city of Jerusalem which was finally declared a United Nations International City. Power was shared by a triumvirate consisting of the Palestinian Chairman, the Prime Minister of Israel and the pope.

In Ireland, the Protestants in the north and the Catholics in the south still attempted to bomb one another into switching religions. Numerous peace treaties were made and broken. Although Catholics and Protestants were encouraged to sing and drink side-by-side in pubs, the evenings usually ended in a ruckus that left shards of broken glass and puddles of beer on the floor.

Although the cold war was ancient history, frequent outbursts of violence occurred in the Balkan states, as well as in Afghanistan, China, Haiti, Indonesia, India, Pakistan, Sri Lanka, and several sub-Saharan African states, to name a few. The U.S. government, showing great restraint, only detached fighting men to areas that were deemed to be in the national interest, meaning oil.

At home in America, racial and ethnic profiling by police and customs agents became punishable by forcing these officials to perform hundreds of hours of community service working in inner city soup kitchens. In retaliation, police and customs agents began targeting middle-aged white males in the hope of snaring the politicians and judges who passed and enforced the laws that ignored what they thought were the real offenders, and branded *them* offenders.

Pentagon generals and admirals were ordered to strip all bells, whistles and gold plate from weapons systems. Seven-hundred dollar toilet seats and three-hundred dollar hammers were eliminated by ordering the Defense Department to make all such purchases at Home Depot or Sears Roebuck, whichever was cheaper.

And to the surprise of some, the consternation of others, but the pleasure of most, America not only survived, but actually thrived under the aegis of its first Jewish president.

Mazel Tov!

YIDDISH EXPRESSIONS

ALEVASHOLEM	May he rest in peace
ALEHA HA-SHALOM	May she rest in peace
BRITH or BRIS	Circumcision ceremony performed eight days after birth
BAR MITZVAH	Ceremony performed in a synagogue when a boy becomes thirteen years old; a confirmation of faith and responsibility
BAS MITZVAH	Similar ceremony for a girl
KNISH	Type of potato pancake
GEVALT	Exclamation of dismay
KVETCH	To complain
MATSO	Unleavened bread
MAZEL TOV	Congratulations
MENSII	A responsible, dignified person
MITVAH	A good deed; a favor
ONEG SHABBAT	Social function; usually with refreshments served after a religious service
OY	All-purpose exclamation to express joy, shock, dismay, pain, relief, indignation
SCHLEP	To walk, usually dragging one's feet

YIDDISH EXPRESSIONS, (Cont'd.)

SHLEMIEL	A born loser; a hard luck type
SHMUCK	Off-color reference to the male appendage
SHOLOM	Hello! or Goodbye!; also: Peace!
TALIS	Prayer shawl
TOCHIS	The fanny
YARMULKE	Skullcap worn by observing Jewish males

About the Author

Tom Clancy is a native of Brooklyn, New York. He attended Wesleyan University in Middletown, Connecticut, the University of Maryland, and Catholic University in Washington, DC, receiving both Bachelor and Master's Degrees.

He served on active duty in the U.S. Navy and later served a full career in the Navy Department. He was a columnist for a Navy newspaper, and authored official Navy newsletters.

Clancy co-authored with LaRee Simon a novel titled *The Ladies of the Wednesday Investment Club*.

He is retired from the Navy and resides in Maryland.

Printed in the United States
122544LV00002B/95/P